My silver fox Bratv
blood and bullets.
And because of one
He demands a pen

CW01501877

It started when Konstar
"accounting mistake."
I'm just a curvy, bookish nobody who wears vintage dresses and tries not to faint when he enters the room.
But he pinned me up against the wall of his office with threats of punishment if I don't tell him who's pulling my strings.

I should never have felt turned on by the heat of his hands.
I should never have melted at the brush of his lips on my neck.
And I should never have accidentally sent him a sext...
Alone in my bed, *thinking* of him.

So imagine my shock the next morning when he murmurs...
"You're going to give me an heir, Miss Wolfe.
And I'm going to give you exactly what you've
been begging for."

Except what starts as punishment quickly turns into a dangerously addictive obsession.

And when he finds out who's using me to get at
him? He'll turn this city's streets into their
grave.

Sexting My Bratva Boss

A Silver Fox Mafia Romance

Mafia Silver Foxes

Sierra Voss

* * *

Chapter 1

Audrey

I can feel his eyes on me.

Konstantin Martynov is not a man you want watching you. Even if you fantasize about the things he could do to you right here in his luxury skyrise.

Konstantin Martynov, mafia boss and billionaire, CEO of not one, but seven companies. Globally.

"Are you okay?"

The question is a hiss, and I lick my lips before turning to face Chrissy, my best friend and co-accountant for Martynov Global Holdings.

"You're...sweating."

She's right. My body is reacting to the fact that *he's* near, and watching me.

Every. Single. Time his eyes have landed on me in the past year, my body *reacts*.

I *should* be afraid. Knees trembling with fear, heart stuttering with anxiety. Instead, a shiver down my spine makes my shoulders roll back, nipples erect and poorly hidden under a satin blouse.

Konstantin Martynov could kill me with a look, but I'm pretty sure he could do other sinful things to me if I ever dared to be alone with him.

"I'm fine, Chris. Just a little warm."

She cocks an eyebrow, graciously not mentioning my breasts as I hug manila folders tightly. "Mmm. This office is air conditioned, Audrey, and kept at a perfect ambient temperature. Are you sure you aren't sick or something?"

Oh, I'm sick alright, because no one should regularly fantasize about their *literally* killer boss. And that's not even taking into consideration the fact that I have a boyfriend.

The timeless *swish* of a tempered glass door opening interrupts us.

The man himself steps into the space, eyes sweeping across dark wood and metal desks and high-end electronics. Only the best for a global criminal enterprise.

Mr. Martynov looks like a fallen angel of the worst kind. His silver hair gleams, grizzled jawline perfectly mirrored by a sharp collar and dark bespoke suit. Four bodyguards back him, each a tower of muscle, tattoos, and silence.

His dark eyes find me and land on my parted lips.

"Good morning Mr. Martynov," the four other accountants murmur demurely, eyes down.

I make the mistake of being unable to look away. All I can hope is that he doesn't see this as a threat, or a challenge, because I'm already in deep. And not just because my panties are damp.

"Good morning ladies." The words rumble from his chest, darkened by his thick accent. He strides slowly across the floor; I'm the only thing standing between Konstantin

Martynov and his office, down a private hallway and guarded at all times.

Taking a step back, the too-thin heel of my Manolos catches on a dropped pen and I stumble, stifling a cry at the pain searing through my ankle.

A large hand shoots out, catching my upper arm and wrenching me up.

Right into Martynov's grip.

His other hand presses my body closer to his. "You're okay?" he asks, voice even and void of emotion as always.

But his eyes flash caramel. I swear the manila folder between us should be bursting into flame with the rush of heat that takes over my body.

"I'm...fine. Thank you, Mr. Martynov."

My gaze drops to the floor. And the stupid dogtooth-patterned heels that got me in this predicament.

He steps away and it's as if the whole room is holding their breath; all the accountants, all four guards, and the poor cleaning woman who is on her way to stock the break room.

"Good. Because as always, Miss Wolfe, I expect you in my office promptly at 10 a.m."

I nod, unable to look up for fear that I'll do something stupid, like damage my ankle even more by letting it give just so I can fall into his arms again.

In a moment, Mr. Martynov and his men are gone— disappeared down the hallway behind double-thick cement walls and bulletproof glass.

"Shit," I murmur, hobbling back to my desk and falling into the chair. Chrissy is at my side immediately, concern and suspicion in her eyes.

"Are you alright?"

"Yeah, I just feel like an idiot."

"Don't worry about it. It was...awkward," her narrow eyes suggest that 'awkward' isn't what she's actually thinking, "but I doubt he'd *kill* you over tripping over a pen, Aud. Is it just me, or was there some tension between you two?"

I shoot her a glare. That's a dangerous thing to whisper in this office. And a man like Konstantin Martynov would never give in to fucking the help, I'm sure.

"No, there most definitely was not. And don't even think about saying that in front of Sal."

Her features twist briefly, and my stomach drops. I know how Chrissy feels about Sal, even if she's never told me to my face. It's easy to see she despises him and can't figure out why I'm with him.

Too bad I can't tell her I've been doubting that decision lately. There are some things that are safer kept to myself.

Like how often I imagine Mr. Martynov stepping in, claiming me, and scaring my boyfriend off. Ugh.

"You have the reports ready, right?"

I flop the folders onto my desk, giving her a half-hearted smile. She returns to her desk with a curious glance over the shoulder, and my own eyes flick to the clock on the wall.

9:45 a.m.

I have fifteen minutes.

Chrissy is right—Konstantin Martynov, ruthless Russian mob boss, wouldn't kill me over stumbling into his path.

But he would if I was stupid enough to put myself in his path by doing something reckless.

Like stealing from the company.

* * *

Two minutes shy of 10 a.m., I stand and gather my things. It's not much, but in the last ten minutes I've set myself back to rights: tucked my hair behind my ears, made sure I smell like the spiced vanilla scent I love and not sweat, and wiggled the heel of my right shoe to make sure it won't snap off.

Chrissy gives me an encouraging smile. Two of the other accountants don't even glance my way; it's a consuming job, making sure the books for Martynov Global Holdings reflect only legal transactions. No hint of the safe-houses, money laundering, or silent auction income anywhere on the lines.

But Duscha rolls her eyes.

It's easy to catch, and expected. She doesn't try to hide her dislike of me. Duscha has been working for Konstantin Martynov for... forever, maybe. She's a Russian immigrant-turned-recent-citizen, and is stunning for a woman of her age. Her features are sharp, skin pale and clear, eyes cutting and hair pin-straight. If she wasn't such a bitch I'd be jealous. Duscha trained me and hated me as soon as she realized that I not only knew what I was doing, but that I was doing it *better* than she was.

Taking a deep breath, I start toward the glass door that separates our room from the hallway that leads to Mr. Martynov. It's only a moment, but Duscha... smiles.

And *that* worries me.

Mr. Martynov's favored guard, a young man named Lev, is sitting outside the door with his legs spread wide and a casual posture. Casual, but I'm pretty sure Lev could tear a man's spine out with his bare hands. He's huge, almost as big as Martynov himself, and also mute. I give him a small smile, but his face doesn't change. He's learned well from his master.

My knock is like music on the high-end glass. Mr. Martynov is standing at the window, staring down at the city. Two fingers on his right-hand twitch, signaling me to enter. I try not to think of how confident that little gesture is, and what else he could use it for.

"Mr. Martynov. I apologize for earlier, and thank you again—"

"No need to thank me, Miss Wolfe."

He turns, his eyes dragging down my body. Once more every inch of my skin reacts to just his *gaze*. It's amazing I didn't combust under his hands earlier.

"What can you tell me about Dubai."

I take my place near his desk and open the top folder, beginning to recite the revenue and expenses of his Dubai projects. Right now, at surface level, it appears that he's close to being in the red; after all, he's building lavish condos that are selling for half what they're worth. But once they're finished, they'll be used as safehouses for criminals escaping Eastern Europe.

I touch briefly on the low-income properties he just put up in the UK and how the head church in the area is so grateful they are willingly laundering his money via donations. Before I can get to the Black Orchid project, he interrupts.

"Down."

"I—what?"

"Sit down."

Hesitantly, I reach out to maneuver a leather chair, but Martynov points at the floor in front of him.

"Not there. Here."

I swallow, and it feels like a stone is stuck in my throat. This time, a cold sweat comes on and the folder trembles in my hand.

"Put that down. If you make me tell you one more time you won't stand back up, Miss Wolfe."

With a quiet gasp, I drop the folder on his desk, take two steps to him, and drop to my knees, biting back the pain as I kneel before him. They'll be bruised later no matter how thick my pencil skirt is.

Konstantin Martynov towers over me. I stare up, trying hard to ignore the fact that my nose could graze his inner thigh and the slight bulge that always makes my mouth water.

"Miss Wolfe." He reaches out. His fingers and thumb wrap around my jaw, squeezing just enough for it to be uncomfortable. "I hired you at the behest of your manager, when my last accountant was unfortunately deemed... dispensable. I can tell you that what she was fired for was nowhere near as grievous as what you've been doing, *zólotse*. So, explain to me why I shouldn't throw a chair through that window and have your delectable little body follow it to break apart on the street below."

The breath catches in my throat. I try to swallow, but my mouth is dry, and tears gather at the corners of my eyes.

This is it.

But... something catches in the back of my mind.

Did he say 'delectable'?

Twisting my fingers together to hide their trembling, I

try to ignore the pool of desire that rushes to my core. I *should not* be turned on right now, not when one of the most dangerous men in the world is threatening to kill me. Even if his thumb is stroking reassuringly along my jaw.

"I don't know what you're talking about."

The words sound brittle, weak. Mr. Martynov smiles. He reaches into the hidden pocket of his suit jacket and removes papers folded in thirds. Before he's even dropped them in front of me, I know what they are.

"It seems you've made an error. Here."

He nudges the papers with his foot, as if pointing, but it's performative and he doesn't have to make his point—I know exactly which line item on the account he's talking about.

Exactly what error.

Because it isn't an error.

"And another one."

Another paper flutters to the ground.

"Last month. And the month before that."

Despite it all I can't help the flash of defiance that I know shows in my eyes.

His own narrows when he notices. Was he expecting me to grovel?

I should; I should beg. I should slit my own throat right here, because a man like Konstantin Martynov won't let anyone get away with this.

"*Vorovka.* You think I don't know that you've been stealing from me? That for *six months* you've been cleaning the accounts and covering your tracks?"

I try to turn away, but he tightens his grip, angling my

face upwards, his thumb pressing on the seam of my lips. He *growled* that word, *vorovka*.

I've been working here long enough to pick up on some Russian. To understand that he caught me.

Vorovka means thief.

The pressure from his massive hand forces my mouth open, and my eyes water as he slowly presses two thick fingers inside. They slide over my tongue, rough and salty, seeking deeper and deeper until I gag and whimper.

"You've made a mistake, Miss Wolfe. But... I think you're smart."

He licks his lips and again my body betrays me. I *hate* that this is turning me on, that being on my knees with my jaw forced open and the taste of his skin on my tongue does this to me.

For a moment, I absolutely *loathe* Konstantin Martynov.

It's just as strong as my lust. And not a new feeling; I've hated Martynov ever since I realized just what Sal, my boyfriend, had gotten me into with that accounting job at the construction site.

Only I never thought it would lead here.

He removes his fingers, shoving me back with a push of his knee. I fall onto my heels, sucking in a deep breath, tears trickling down my cheeks and into my mussed hair. They run down my neck and soak into the satin blouse.

"The problem is, if you're as smart as I think you are, you would never steal from me. Which means you must have a very good reason for doing such a stupid thing. And you're going to tell me right now."

Chapter 2

Konstantin

The clasp of my belt *snicks* open and I watch her eyes widen. It makes my cock stir, the way she fears me; the way I can tell she's torn between scrambling away from me or submitting, giving up those luscious lips for my use.

It's tempting.

I've been fantasizing about wrecking Audrey Wolfe ever since she set foot in my office.

Before that, even. Ever since I saw her at that job site and told Olena I wanted her transferred. Wanted her closer.

Wanted to feast my eyes on her body every day.

Those plump curves, the prim clothes she wears. Tight dresses with high collars and stockings with the lines up the back. Makes me wonder if she has a garter belt pressing into her thick hips and what kind of sounds she'd make if I snapped it.

I want to *devour* her.

I want to own her.

And she's finally given me the way to make that happen.

"I want you to stand up, Miss Wolfe."

Taking a step back, I can't help smirking as her eyes narrow and lips purse. She wants to curse me, I'm sure, because standing up on those precarious heels of hers will be hard to do.

She gets one foot under her, wobbles, and falls forward, grabbing my thighs. The trousers I had pressed only yesterday are getting wrinkled under her clenched hands and my cock twitches with interest again.

"If you're trying to distract me by undressing me, it won't work, Miss Wolfe."

She glowers up at me, but her cheeks go pink. Pressing her palms to the floor, she gets her balance and stands, arms crossed over her chest.

I tip my chin toward the desk.

"There."

"What..." She glances at the desk, solid dark wood, and then back at me apprehensively. "What do you want me to--?"

"Bend over," I interrupt.

The leather belt is warm in my hand. Audrey seems to realize what I'm demanding, and her eyes widen, but she takes tentative steps toward the desk, obeying.

Good.

I need to know that she can do as I say. Even if it scares her.

She puts her hands on the desk and bends over, but her back is rigid, hair spilling over her shoulders. She glances back at me wildly.

"Mm mmm." Gently but firmly, I nudge her feet wider apart with a boot.

Her breathing picks up.

But she can't help it; her lower back arches, giving me her ass, encased perfectly in the beige pencil skirt that hugs every curve.

I lick my lips, the leather belt sliding through my hand as I get ready to punish her.

Then Lev clears his throat.

There's no mistaking it, because the sounds that come out of Lev are primal and grating. He has never once spoken; not since my men picked him up on the street when he was seven years old and beaten half to death.

He has a tongue but doesn't use it.

I've thought many times that the young man could be made to speak in tongues if the right woman fucked him. But what my soldiers get up to in their free time is entirely their business.

"What."

He gives me a bored look, but the twitch of his eyebrow tells me something is up. Most likely on home turf, since Lev heads the soldiers in this city.

He knows he's dismissed as soon as I look away, and disappears silently.

Audrey lets out a shuddering breath. It's delicious; stepping forward, I press my hips to her ass, reach around, and wrap her throat with one hand. All it takes is a little pressure for her to whimper.

She's *mine*.

"Miss Wolfe," I whisper in her ear, smirking as she presses her ass to my already-throbbing dick, "I'm going to make you pay me back, one way or another. And you'll tell me who made you do this—whether I have to get it out of you in a scream or a moan."

A shiver runs down her spine as I release her and step away.

She grabs her folders, weak-kneed, and can't meet my eyes as she hurries from the office.

If I'm right, then as much as Miss Wolfe hates me, she'll spend the day pressing her thighs together and wishing I was fucking her over this very desk.

There's a thin line between hate and lust.

"*Blyat'.*" Shit.

Eyes closed, I rub my palm over my member, knowing that it'll be impossible to sleep now that I'm aware of what her body feels like pressed tightly against mine.

It takes a deep breath or two before I'm calm enough to summon Lev. A button on my desk buzzes him, and he slips back into the room.

"I want you to follow her."

Like a good soldier, he doesn't question me. Never has. Lev stares in that unblinking way of his, which unnerves everyone he comes across as much as his silence.

"Discreetly," I add, rounding the desk to sit in the high-backed chair. "She's lying about why she took the money, and I want to know why. A woman like Miss Wolfe doesn't make stupid fucking decisions unless she's afraid."

Anger boils through me. Flexing my clenched fist, I try to fight the urge to walk out onto the floor again, tower over her, and demand to know who's controlling her.

Because she's *mine.* Mine to control. And I'll kill any man who makes her feel threatened.

Lev doesn't look convinced. There are only a handful of times in my life I've felt the need to explain myself. With my position and power, explanations would be seen as a weakness; as the need to justify my actions.

I'm not that kind of man.

I do what I want, *take* what I want, and leave others to deal with the fallout.

But Lev has a way of making me think out loud. And I know he'd never say a word to anyone about my musings, so I lean back and expound.

"I'll get the truth out of her and punish her for taking what's mine. And then I'll hunt down whoever put her up to it and destroy them."

Lev slips his phone out of his pocket, deftly typing up a succinct request: access to her employee information, questions about how many men I want on her place, and what to do if someone shows up.

I make it clear that I want blood, but that ultimately, I want the kill.

And that they should do anything in their power to protect her.

Then I try to turn my attention back to the matter at hand: running my empire.

The one I worked so hard for.

The one I intend to keep.

The townhouse is five floors, with a bar on the roof and a pool on the lower level. Every inch of it screams luxury, and every inch has been tailored to my needs.

Somehow, it isn't satisfying me tonight.

I pace the third floor and look out across the river. It's dark, city lights shimmering on the surface.

I've put countless bodies in that water.

I'll put thousands more in before I'm done.

And yet... it all feels purposeless.

With a low growl, I slide the glass of kvass across the table and stalk out of the room.

The drink is cheap; sweet and sour, with a heady scent that reminds me of bread. Specifically, of the breadbox in my mother's home, the one painted with little red flowers. I close my eyes and I'm there again: Russia thirty years ago, stomach growling as I tuck myself into the corner of the kitchen and hope there's food for the night.

The memory drives me to my own kitchen. It takes up half of the first floor, industrial-style prep tables and high-end appliances gleaming black and steel. A wall of knives, more than my personal chef will ever need, and a refrigerator that's as big as a restaurant's walk-in.

I'll never go hungry here.

I've made sure of that.

"So why isn't this enough?" I hiss, gripping the cold steel table and feeling the pulsing echo of the hole in my chest.

Thirty years.

Thirty years ago, I climbed out of that hell-hole. Thirty years ago, I promised my mother I'd come back for her, that I'd make her life better.

And I did.

But she sent me away; didn't want me. Even after I moved her and her *svoloch'* second husband to a real home, a two-story in the city center with heat and water and groceries delivered once a week.

Even then she didn't want me.

So, this is my home now—America. I've built an empire on this asphalt, expanded further than I ever imagined. My reach knows no bounds. This very week I have men negotiating in China for a megatower, connecting our arms deal to the far east.

It's what I should be thinking about, that deal, and the expansion of my holdings.

Instead, I'm picturing *her*. Spread out on this very table, nipples hard from the cold steel, soft skin rippling with pleasure as I pound into her over and over.

As I make her beg, for forgiveness, for more, for mercy.

Audrey Wolfe.

Dropping my head into my hands, I try to fight off the snippets of her that my mind has saved up. Later, alone in the shower, they'll come back. I'll fist my cock to fantasies of yanking one of those little dresses up, exposing her ass, making her cry out as the belt leaves a red mark.

She needs to be punished.

No longer plagued by thoughts of my childhood, I return to the study and pull open a drawer. Inside is a folder —one given to me by Duscha, so loyal and conniving, so jealous and ambitious.

It was she who noticed Audrey's mistake. Not that it's her job to check the other accountants' work.

I never trusted her, she'd snarled in my office when everyone had gone home. She'd begged a meeting with me via Olena, who I was surprised gave in and agreed.

Women.

Always trying to destroy one another.

Little did Duscha know, she gave me the very thing I needed to bring Miss Wolfe *closer*. To get a tighter grip on her.

"What am I going to do with you?" I murmur, turning a page slowly to stare down at her personnel file.

Her home address is listed there, an apartment. Small, probably, but good enough. Something for her to be proud of.

"I could give you so much more."

But first... she needs to be punished.

She needs to give me what I'm owed. Or I can take it from her.

Somewhere in the office my phone buzzes dully. I find it hidden beneath today's suit jacket, but it's not my personal phone; it's my business phone.

The one with every important employee's number in it.

The one for emergencies.

Her full name and position appear atop the message:
Audrey Lauren Wolfe, Head Accountant.

The message itself... well, it has my attention. And makes it even more clear that I need to break her.

Watch her eyes fill with hate as I fill her with my seed.

Audrey Wolfe will give me what I really want.

A child.

Chapter 3

Audrey

"**A**re you up for going to Sottovoce? I could use something to take the edge off."

Chrissy pauses on the sidewalk, a look of surprise on her face. "Really? You *never* want to go out after work."

"Well, that's because I don't exactly enjoy talking about Excel spreadsheets with Jeanette, Grace, and Duscha."

She gives me an apologetic smile and steps up to the curb to flag a taxi. Mr. Martynov isn't an idiot; his stronghold is located on the far side of the city, away from the Italian section and Sottovoce—the bar I met Sal at.

"Do you really think Duscha had something to do with getting you in trouble?"

"Where to?" the driver interrupts as we slide into the backseat of the cab. Chrissy gives him a curt response, just enough time for me to process how to respond. She knows that Mr. Martynov was *not* happy with me, but I couldn't tell her why.

Chrissy's been my best friend since I started as a head

accountant for Martynov Global Holdings a year ago. Before that, I was the accountant for one of Mr. Martynov's construction offshoots—a grimy job that Sal got me not too long after my grandmother died, when I was unmoored and scared I'd lose her house.

Turns out I did anyway.

Forehead pressed against the cool glass of the window, I stare up at the Obsidian Spire—Martynov's NYC head-quarters and the place we work, all the way up on the 28th floor.

Chrissy nudges me with concern.

"I don't know," I sigh. "I think so, yeah. I... made an error in an account, and Duscha must have caught it and told him. She gave me such a shit-eating smirk when I came out of his office."

I wrap my arms around myself, remembering the fear and desire coursing through me as I walked stiffly back to my desk. My ankle still pulsed with a bruise from tripping, and then the strain of kneeling before him.

Submitting.

"She's always been a bitch," Chrissy mutters. "Although I have no idea why she's snooping in your assignments. I wonder if she's been in the rest of ours, too."

The cab cuts through the back streets as Chris continues to chat, mostly complaining about the complexity of handling the Eastern European accounts and the headaches she's been getting at night.

This is what I like most about her; Chrissy lets me just... exist. It was exactly what I needed after Nana passed, and it was part of what made me give in to Sal's pursuit as well. It was so easy to give up control then when I was grieving. So easy to let someone tell me what to do, or to let them talk about their day mindlessly as I floated in the foggy loss.

But Nana has been gone for a long time now.

And it's hitting me just how dangerous what Sal has me doing is; just how close I've come to burning up like a moth in a flame.

The only thing keeping me safe is the fact that Mr. Martynov wants to toy with me.

And that he wants an answer as to why I would steal close to $50K. The thing is, he's right; normally I'm not that stupid. I did it because I *have* to.

The *ping* of Chrissy paying our fare rouses me, and I follow her out of the cab and onto the street. It's early fall and even though the trees aren't changing color yet, it's darker earlier. A chilly breeze makes me shiver as we hurry into Sottovoce.

Inside isn't much better; Sottovoce is dimly lit, a classy wine bar of leather and velvet, whispers, and trysts. The first time Sal brought me here I found it exciting and took Chrissy here a few times after work... before I realized that this is actually a front for Giuseppe Sartorre, Mr. Martynov's competition, and leader of the Italian mob.

"Miss Wolfe," the bartender greets us, "Miss Lin."

He gives Chrissy those Italian stallion bedroom eyes, and I almost roll mine, then hope to God she isn't actually falling for it.

The last thing I need is for *her* to get mixed up between crime syndicates, too, since I can barely keep myself safe.

"Two glasses of white, please," I snap, and he eyes me up darkly.

"Mr. Imperi isn't here tonight, Miss Wolfe. But I can let him know you stopped by."

His words are cold.

They make my heart stutter.

I don't want to see Sal tonight, not just because I'm pissed at the danger he's put me in.

I'm also... scared of him.

And I hate that.

Chrissy glances at me over the rim of her glass. When the bartender moves away just a bit, she asks, "Want to grab a booth? A bit more privacy?"

I nod, carefully pick up the stem glass, and the two of us wind our way across the bar to a corner booth. Sinking into the seat, the scent stirs something in me... the smell of leather.

Mr. Martynov's belt in his hand.

The way he bent me over the desk, lingered behind me like a predator.

I take a shaky sip, and then another. "I really, really don't want to see Sal tonight. Sorry—is it okay if we make this quick?"

"Yeah, of course. But Audrey... it seems like things haven't been going great between you two. Maybe it's time to break it off?"

The wine buzzes on my tongue as I let it warm in my mouth, shaking my head. "Mm. Trust me. That would be more disastrous than just avoiding him."

Chrissy snorts. "He can't be *that* good in bed, Aud, even if he is pretty."

That makes me laugh. "You're right. Actually, Sal is

kind of... um, selfish is the nice way to put it, I guess. Or focused. But only on himself."

"Aren't they all," Chrissy mutters, and we both giggle into our glasses.

"I don't know," I sigh, leaning back. "It might be a bit complicated to end things with him now when everything at work is getting messy. I need Mr. Martynov to trust me again and not fire me."

"He would never, Aud. There's a *reason* you were promoted, you know."

"Yeah, well, if Duscha can keep her job with that sour look she always has on her face, maybe I have a chance."

"I don't know why she has it out for you. Have you ever said anything bad about her? To Mr. Martynov?"

"No, never. Trust me, we barely talk when I'm in that office. Or at least he barely talks. I run through the report, keep my eyes on the papers, and then he gestures for me to leave. That's it."

Chrissy smirks.

I know what's coming even before she says it, because Chrissy has had this theory for so long.

"I think he went easy on you because he's got a thing for you, Audrey. You know—a little *forbidden office romance* on the mind."

I can't help smiling, it's such a ridiculous idea.

"You're reading too many of those books. Trust me, a man like Konstantin Martynov isn't at all interested in *romance*."

"Okay. That's still not a problem though, right? I mean, if you just have to fuck your way out of this problem, there are worse things."

"Chris!"

I lunge across the booth, tipsily moving to cover her mouth with my hand as she cackles. We're drawing attention from the bartender as well as the patrons that have started to settle into nooks and tables.

The wine caught up to me faster than I realized. For starters, I'm terrified that the bartender really might've let Sal know I'm here, and that he'll appear at any moment and hear Chrissy talking about me fucking my boss.

That would *not* go over well. Sal has been... volatile lately. And while it hasn't escalated to physical fights yet, the last time he was over he smashed one of my Nana's Roseville Dogwood vases. It was priceless, both in terms of actual money and nostalgia. I cried for days.

"Okay, I think we're done here," I chastise, but give her a smile so she knows I'm not actually mad.

More than anything I'm distracted.

By thoughts of my boss... because what are the chances that Chris is right? What else would explain why he let me walk out of his office today, knowing I've stolen from him?

No one steals from Konstantin Martynov.

Which means he's brainstorming a new level of punishment for me, or Chris is right, and he has a soft spot for me.

Forty-five minutes later, I step into my apartment and wobble a bit.

"Fuck off," I mutter, kicking off the heels that betrayed me this morning.

My apartment is small and dark except for a little lamp

throwing amber light across the living room. I love how homey and calm it makes me feel immediately and start to undo the zipper of my pencil skirt, which it now feels like I'm going to burst out of.

Just in crossing the room I manage to peel off most of my clothes, leaving me in only the silk panties and matching bra I slipped into this morning. Going into the kitchen, I rummage around for girl dinner—pretty much whatever I can find, since it's already after 7 p.m.

Leaning against the kitchen counter to eat cold cuts and crackers, I'm reminded once again of Konstantin bending me over his desk.

Mr. Martynov.

Ugh, I can't start thinking of him by his first name—I'm pretty sure if I slip and call him "Konstantin" to his face it'll be just as bad as the missing $50K.

Only that money isn't missing.

It's Sal's now.

With a groan, I drop my head onto the counter. "What am I going to do?" I whisper.

Somehow, I've found myself stuck between two criminal organizations. It's so ridiculous that I laugh, and then immediately tear up, because if Nana could see me now—I can already imagine the disappointment on her face.

I did it for you. I just wanted you to be comfortable in those last few months.

Banishing the guilt, I open the refrigerator again and find an old bottle of Riesling. Old enough that when I take a swig, it's sour-vinegary and overpowering. But tonight, I don't want to think about Nana and how she struggled at the end.

I don't want to think about the possibility of my *own* ending, possibly at the hands of my murderous boss.

Frustrated, tipsy, and angry at the world, I march over to my purse and dig around for my cellphone.

This is a bad decision.

Snorting, I ignore the voice of reason in the back of my head and scroll down to a number I've never texted before. The contact's name is: Last Resort.

A warning.

This is Konstantin Martynov's direct number, only to be used if we are ever caught by his rivals. Threatened. Tortured.

A way to let him know they're coming for him.

The funny thing is, most people in Martynov's organization have this number.

But every single one of them are too afraid to use it for anything other than... a last resort.

Finger hovering over Last Resort, I lick my lips. It feels like my body is a kettle that's been boiling all day, and I need to blow off steam.

Before I can open a new text message, a notification flashes at the top of the screen.

It's a message from Sal.

What the hell did you do, *piccolo idiota?*

Little idiot. That's his newest nickname for me.

Refusing to respond, I instead tap on Last Resort and type out a quick, angry message, fueled by wine, anger, fear —and the warmth that's still pooling between my thighs at the thought of Konstantin standing over me.

If you're going to threaten to debauch me, the least you

could do is follow through. Maybe you're too busy running a global empire to satisfy a woman.

My nipples pebble in the cool air of the apartment as I hit send, and then grow bolder:

I guess I'll just have to take care of it myself.

Sliding the phone across the counter, I slip my hand beneath the silk panties and find my throbbing clit easily. As soon as my fingers graze it, I whimper; a sound mirroring the one I made in Konstantin's office with his erection pressed against my ass.

Eyes closed, I let the fantasy play out beyond the guard's interruption:

'I'm going to make you pay me back, one way or another.'

What would he have done next? Yanked up my skirt and spanked me until my skin was red and raw?

Undone his zipper and fisted himself, rubbing his hard length between my folds?

'You'll tell me who made you do this.'

Trying to mimic the way I want him to touch me, I let out another frustrated whimper; my slim fingers are no match for Konstantin Martynov's large hands and rough touch. But after a day of feeling on edge, turned on, and in danger, the wine is all I need to loosen up just enough...

'Whether I have to get it out of you in a scream or a moan.'

The orgasm washes over me hard, a ripple from my center to the hard peaks of my nipples, shudders running through me with my legs spread and the sloppy sounds of my desire filling the little apartment as I ride it out on my fingers.

It takes a moment to catch my breath.

Across the counter, my phone lights up.

Sal has probably heard from someone about the incident in the Spire. I know he has a mole inside, someone other than me, but I haven't been able to figure out why. Either way, he'll be pissed that I'm on Martynov's radar now.

Sighing, I tap the screen.

The notification is from Chrissy asking if I got back okay, since we took separate cabs. I start to type back, but then see the three little dots on another text thread—

The message to Last Resort.

The dirty, pushy, snappy challenge I sent to my boss only minutes ago. I brace myself for his response, but there isn't one.

The three little dots disappear.

Under my message is the small phrase **Read 7:45 p.m.**

Fuck.

With a man like Konstantin Martynov, silence is a death sentence.

Chapter 4

Konstantin

Unlike in movies, the security center of the Obsidian Spire isn't in the basement. It isn't dark, damp, or locked behind thick walls of concrete.

I need my men to have access at all times.

I need to have access at all times.

"Move."

The guard doesn't make eye contact or even flinch, as if it's a normal occurrence for me to appear on the second floor, where the Command Center is located, and usurp his chair. It's well-worn and comfortable, made for hours of sitting in front of these monitors, which take up most of the sixteen-foot wall. He stands, gathers the coffee mug and radio, and steps away.

Lev has cleared everyone else out. He remains at the main door with his back facing me as he stares out through the glass.

The door is one of five that allow my guards out into the building, giving them the fastest access possible.

The walls are all glass-clad polycarbonate; bulletproof and ensuring that every single person who enters this building beyond the first floor is observed.

My eyes scan the TVs quickly. It takes me a moment to find, but there she is—Audrey Wolfe, entering the building at 8 a.m. on the dot.

I smirk.

It's easier to track her now that I have my bearings. She scans in, walks through the two security checkpoints, greets someone, continues to the escalator. It will bring her to this floor, where she'll walk right by this office.

And she does.

I turn the chair and watch.

She's wearing kitten heels today, either worried about tripping again or dealing with a sore ankle.

Lev has turned half-away to make himself less obvious. He glances at me, and I know he notices, too, the difference in her appearance.

Her dark hair looks frizzy instead of sleek and perfectly styled. No form fitting skirt, no stockings, no deliciously tempting neckline; she's wearing a dress that flares out at the hips and almost reaches her ankles.

This is the first sign that I might be in trouble: if I only wanted her for her looks, I'd be bothered. But there's something about the outfit, the way it hides her curves and bare skin, that makes me want to explore her even more.

She marches past the Command Center and disappears to the elevators.

"Come," I say quietly, standing and leading the way out of the room. As Lev steps out behind me, the regular security staff file back in efficiently. I wait thirty feet from the elevators, but Audrey never looks up once she's inside one. She stares at the ground.

I can't help smirking. It's easy to see she's nervous, disheveled, most likely by yesterday's events...

And the dirty text she sent me last night.

The doors close and I gesture for Lev to follow. We take the stairs, quickly, easily. He might be almost twenty years younger than me, but I'm not a fool; in my line of work, it's important to stay in shape.

To kill time, I stop on the eight floor and check in with my suppliers. It's a rare visit, and they're nervous, suspecting that something is wrong. The pretty little secretary out front flutters her fake lashes at me. I barely give her a second glance.

Minutes later, figuring Audrey is most likely settled in the office, Lev and I take the elevator. When the doors open the four employees inside scatter quickly and quietly. Stepping inside, I focus on the numbers lighting up slowly.

Just the thought of seeing her today has me worked up. It takes a moment to control my breath, to relax my muscles.

I want to hunt her like the prey animal she is.

We reach the final floor of the Obsidian Spire, where the three most important divisions are: accounting, international affairs, and leadership.

And of course, my office.

"Good morning, Mr. Martynov," the accounting girls demure—

All but Audrey.

She's rummaging in her desk, computer screen black, a flush on her cheeks.

My smirk widens.

Striding down the hall and to my office, I wait until the door is closed before hitting the button that frosts an internal layer of glass.

Another flicked switch brings up a small screen that looks out onto the three divisions. Quickly, I navigate to the scene I want to see: Audrey, still fumbling, caught off guard by one of the other women asking her a question.

Lev's thumb roams effortlessly across his phone's surface, and a deep, masculine, generated voice speaks: "Is there a problem I can take care of for you?"

"No."

Lev takes a step back.

The growl in my voice surprises me as well, but I keep concentrating on the screen, too absorbed in watching the way Audrey slips her heels off and massages her ankle. Then she glances over her shoulder.

What I don't say is:

This is **my** problem. Something only I'll be able to handle.

"Bring me Miss Wolfe."

On screen, she licks her lips. I like it, so I add: "In another hour. Let her sweat first."

Like the good soldier he is, Lev turns and leaves without a comment.

An hour later he appears on the screen. Audrey is startled by him at her side, and when he doesn't speak, she's even more unnerved.

But she follows him.

I gently stroke the key that unlocks my office door when I can see her shadow out in the hallway. Lev remains out there.

She slips in carefully, and up close she's even more beautiful. Dark hair mussed, eyes tired, lips bitten with nerves.

"Sit."

Her hesitation makes me smile.

"In a chair this time, Miss Wolfe."

Audrey wobbles, but obeys, eyes on the ground as she slowly lowers herself into the Chesterfield chair. It cradles her body in a way that makes me jealous.

I'm out from behind the desk so fast she flinches, and it's delicious.

The closer I get to her, circling behind the chair, the more I can catch her scent: Citrus and vanilla. It makes my mouth water.

Makes me want to devour her.

"Miss Wolfe," I whisper, leaning down until my lips graze her ear, "I believe you were a bad girl last night. Talking to your boss that way... *insubordination,* isn't it, when you decide not to obey."

She takes a shaky breath.

"I... Mr. Martynov, I apologize... I drank a little too much wine and—"

"Isn't there a saying—that the truth comes out when people drink?"

The flush I noticed earlier is back, crawling beautifully up her neck, out from beneath the high collar of her cream dress.

"So, tell me, Miss Wolfe. Did you mean what you said?

That you don't think a man like me has the time to satisfy a woman?"

Her tongue darts out to wet her lips.

It's too much for me, and I grip her jaw from behind, tilting her head upwards carefully until our eyes meet. She's breathing little pants, hitching her breasts up, making me want to rip this prim dress off her body.

"Unfortunately, you didn't give me the chance to prove you wrong. But I wonder... did you go through with your threat?"

Rounding the chair, I shove it back, the sound scraping across the floor.

Lev knows better than to come in. He knows I can handle myself, even against a woman as vexing as this.

Slowly, I kneel in front of her, my hands covering hers where they grip the chair.

"Did you touch yourself?"

When her lips purse tight, I jerk the chair again.

"You know who I am Miss Wolfe. Don't make me ask you again."

She gasps, but answers quickly: "Yes! Y-yes, I did. I... touched myself after sending that text."

With a low rumble, I grip her ankles before sliding my hands slowly up her calves.

She's trembling under my touch.

"And what did you think about, while you had your fingers in that pretty pussy?"

"I—I thought about," her eyes flash, feet planting more firmly, "I thought about how much I *despise you.*"

All at once I want to destroy her, own her, lose myself in her. And teach her a lesson.

Yanking the skirt of her dress up, I dig my fingers into her thigh, massaging and nudging them apart.

"You despise me."

"I do."

She chokes the words out, but her chin is tipped up, defiant.

"Mmm. So, you were thinking of me."

"What?"

She gasps again as I pull her panties down her legs, ripping through them when I reach her knees. They're tossed somewhere off to the left.

"You thought of me. While you touched yourself. You thought of me doing... what?"

"I—"

Her eyes are glued to me as I grip her thighs and lift them, pulling the chair and her closer and placing her legs over my shoulders. She tries once to squeeze her knees together but at my growl she ceases, letting me press a kiss and then a bite to her inner thigh.

Then I smack her ass.

Or as much of it as I can reach in this position.

"Ow!"

It's a reaction, not a marker of real pain. I know because I can smell her desire now, the musky scent of her only inches away. Another kiss, then another—

And I reach her center.

"Tell me what you thought of," I murmur, letting my beard tickle her delicate skin.

Audrey whimpers.

"I thought of you—of us, here—of the way you bent me over the desk and, and..."

She stutters to a stop as I lick short and fast, just once, right over her bud. Audrey's knees shake, bending to pull me closer.

There's no more talking. I bury my face in her pussy, feeling how soaked she is without even having to do much. I knead her thighs, grip them tightly enough to leave bruises later, and suck her clit until her cries are half-pleasure, half-pain.

Then I stop.

Right when she's about to come.

I can tell because her body goes stiff as I pull away and stand. Audrey's eyes are wide, her pupil's blown out and dark, mouth open as she pants.

Embarrassed, she pulls her legs together and tries to sit up in the chair. Through the creamy material of her dress, I can see the peaks of her nipples, begging for attention.

"Stand up."

She does.

Finally, she understands.

She's mine.

"No," I bark sharply as she moves to retrieve her underwear. "Leave them."

Taking her arm firmly, I walk her to the door, knowing that her thighs are drenched. I can still smell her—on my face, in my beard, in this room.

Her hand is on the handle, but I stop her with a whisper.

"I want you to think about this all day, Miss Wolfe. About just how easily I could have made you come. It's nothing to me; it's as easy as pulling a trigger. When you go home tonight, you'll touch yourself again, and you'll think of *this*. Of the way I had you in this chair. Understand?"

She nods, head falling back involuntarily, ass pressing toward me.

She wants more. Good. If she's desperate, she'll do as I say.

"I've thought about what your punishment will be for stealing from me, Miss Wolfe."

Over her shoulder, her scared eyes meet mine.

"You'll give me an heir."

Chapter 5

Audrey

Friday.

Friday comes and I... haven't.

I've been too scared to do what Konstantin told me to do—to touch myself and think of him, of the things he did to me in that room with everyone right down the hall.

Scared because of how much I liked it.

Scared because it was the best almost-sex I've ever had.

And because the man who got me so wet they'll probably have to reupholster that chair is my *boss* and no less than a murderer.

There's a thud out in the hallway, as if I summoned the man himself. I jump, hand to my chest, and stare at the double bolted lock. What are the chances Konstantin decided he's sick of me? That it would be easier to dispose of me than have me carry his child, a surrogate slave to be used as he sees fit?

Cautiously, I walk over, barefoot. Peering through the

peephole doesn't make me feel any more relieved when I see who it is.

Sal.

Damn. I've been avoiding him all week, but there was no escaping this. I'd *had* to tell him what happened, and that meant admitting that Konstantin Martynov found the missing money.

"Oh, God, it's just you."

"Just me. *Just me.* We know who you thought it was, right? Who you're afraid of? You think he's going to send someone to pick you off?"

I bite my lip, not wanting to admit that I *was* scared of that. It wouldn't be hard for Martynov's men to overpower me and make it look like an accident, or a suicide.

"You're out of your fucking mind," Sal hisses, pacing my small apartment as I bolt the lock again.

I hate that he's here, but after avoiding him all week, I couldn't exactly tell him no.

No one tells Sal Imperi no; at least, that's what he tells me every time he pulls his hand back and threatens to leave me black and blue.

He wouldn't do it... or... I don't *think* he'd do it. Too many people would notice, especially Mr. Martynov, now that I have his attention, and Sal doesn't like that.

Sal's scared—probably more scared than I am.

"He's watching you now, you know that? How the hell am I supposed to get what I need from you if Konstantin Martynov is watching you?"

He stops at the window, peeking down at the street below as if Martynov's men are down there right now. They aren't...

Right?

"It's fine," I say, trying to lean casually against my kitchen counter and appease him. I just want something solid between us, because Sal is *pissed*.

"It's fine!? It's fine!? You understand that if he's watching you, it means you can't get into the operations room?"

"He thinks it's an accounting error, Sal. That I'm an idiot, that's all."

I can see the war happening behind his eyes—*he* wants nothing more than to believe I'm an idiot, but he knows better. That's why he picked me. That's why he chose me to infiltrate Martynov's Obsidian Spire.

"Maybe if you hadn't had me steal all that money, he wouldn't have caught on!"

I can't help the burst of angry words; I've been pent up all week, afraid to touch myself and dying to all at the same time. Turns out being incredibly horny can also make you a real bitch, even if your gangster boyfriend walks around with a Glock on his hip.

Sal marches across the room, knocking over a vase of flowers that I bought myself as he goes. The way it shatters should make me flinch, but this is the fourth vase I've bought, and it came from the thrift store. I learned my lesson a few months ago.

"You wouldn't have had to steal the money if you hadn't borrowed it in the first place, would you?"

A shiver goes up my spine, but nothing like the shiver that Konstantin gives me. It isn't a thrill I feel when Sal threatens me. It's disgust. He sounds like a hyena, voice higher the angrier he gets.

I hate him.

I might hate him more than I hate Konstantin Martynov.

If I hadn't met Sal, I wouldn't be in this mess.

If I hadn't had to pay for Nana's home hospice care...

"I can get it," I choke out as he leans over the counter. I'll say anything to get him to leave. "If he's keeping me there it's because I'm important, right? Because I'm...worth something."

His eyes narrow, and I quickly correct myself: "Because he knows I'm good at what I do—hiding his money."

Sal turns away, running a hand through his thick hair.

He's pretty; a classic Italian boy, well-muscled around the shoulders but you can tell he likes food too much. His trousers are pressed, and his button-down shirt is open, flapping against an undershirt stained with sweat despite the autumn weather.

"Sal, I... I can't keep skimming money."

His arm sweeps over the counter, sending a water glass, jar of kitchen utensils, and spice rack over. They crash to the floor. I press myself back against the refrigerator, praying for this storm to end.

"I *need* that money, Audrey," he hisses, stalking toward me. He reached out and, despite being the same height as I am, wraps a hand around my throat.

Tight.

So tight I immediately can't get a breath in, and my own hand locks over his wrist.

"Sa—"

I can't say his name, the air leaving my windpipe in a short burst. "Saa—"

"*I need that money, Audrey.* You fucked me over with this. You fucked up."

He brings his other hand up.

Wraps it around my throat and squeezes.

Something grinds, something that feels like bone.

I let out a hiss of a whimper and my leg kicks, uncontrolled, knocking into the garbage that goes sideways. It immediately smells like trash in the small apartment. Sal curses, stepping away quickly to avoid dirtying his shoes.

It's enough of an imbalance for me to stumble out of his grip.

I make it to the door, but he slams me against it hard. One of my fingers is crushed awkwardly on my left hand and I cry out.

Sal is pressed against me, his body sweaty and smelling of garlic and car leather and cigarettes. I cry out again, desperate, and sure that *this is it.*

Only minutes ago, I was afraid that Konstantin Martynov was sending someone to end me, but that... that would be more merciful than this, I'm sure.

Sal presses my head hard against the door, but he takes too much pleasure in my pain. I manage to get the lock undone and pull back hard, almost opening the door.

It slams shut loudly when he shoves forward again.

"You bitch!"

"Miss Wolfe?"

The voice is recognizable, but I'm dizzy and can't place it. My finger throbs, as do the toes of one foot; Sal must've trampled on them at some point, or maybe I stubbed my foot against the door. He's pulling my head back by my hair when I cry out again.

"Miss Wolfe!"

Someone pushes on the other side of the door. It catches Sal off guard and we both stumble back, the door opening to reveal one of my neighbors—a man named Bill who lives two doors down.

There are grocery bags spilled open in the hallway. He looks brave and scared and horrified all at once, glasses askew as he takes in the sight of Sal holding me up by my hair and a scrape on my face bleeding.

"I'm calling the police."

Sal releases me, suddenly all appeasement as Bill pulls out his phone and quickly dials.

"Woah, woah, man, no need to do that. My girl and I were just having an argument. She disobeyed me—you know how it—"

He doesn't get to finish the sentence. Bill, who stands a good six inches over both of us, glares into the apartment at Sal as I cradle my arms around myself and try to hide. Anywhere, just away from Sal's wild gaze.

"Yes, I'd like to report domestic abuse. No... no, the victim lives here, but I don't think the perpetrator does. Yes. We're at 147 Magnolia, fourth floor. I can try to hold him if—"

Before he can finish, Sal is out the door, slipping by Bill like it's nothing. Bill shouts after him and I hear the thud of Sal's heavy boots down the hallway but, sinking to the ground, I'm dizzy all over again.

"Hey."

Bill is kneeling next to me.

"Hey, Miss Wolfe. Audrey, sorry. Are you okay? They're asking if you need an ambulance—"

I shake my head, finding my voice, although it's hoarse. "No... no thank you. Sorry, please no. Just let him go. He won't come back."

I promise that a few times, though I'm not sure if it's true. Bill gives in eventually and opts to go meet the cops outside when they arrive, their lights flashing down on the street and lighting up the apartment ceiling.

I lock both bolts again, slide down onto the floor, try to catch my breath.

My throat is raw.

Everything feels raw.

What the hell am I doing?

Eyes closed, I see Nana's face—

And it's disapproving.

Thank God she never met Sal. When I started seeing him, he knew about Nana. He's the one who offered me the money for her home hospice care, so she wouldn't have to leave the house.

The house that I lost soon after she passed.

The money that he never explained was a debt, not a gift.

I still owe him thirty grand. And the interest—information from Obsidian Spire, specifically the Operations room.

Tears well out of the corners of my eyes despite how tightly they're shut. *How* did I get here? I was happy once. I felt safe, and carefree.

My phone buzzes.

I don't want to look at it, but I've been ignoring Sal's texts all week. After this... there's no more ignoring him.

Dumb whore, flashes across the screen, followed

43

quickly by another message: **He owns you now. And I'll take you both down. Your debt is doubled.**

The tears come harder, faster. This all feels like a pit I can't get out of—Sal threw me into it, but Konstantin Martynov pulled me down with him.

Down to the very bottom.

Sal's right; I'm his now.

Standing on weak legs, I manage to get to the bathroom, down some Tylenol, and clean up the scrape on my face. It's not as bad as it looks. My scalp pulses with pain and the toes on my right foot are raw. My finger, too, is badly swollen already. Hopefully, it isn't broken; I can't venture out of the apartment, not tonight, so I opt instead for taping it to my middle finger and hoping for the best.

A knock on the door comes just minutes after I manage to look a bit presentable... for a woman who just got beat up. It's a pair of cops, and they ask about Sal—his name, what happened, if I want to press charges. I can feel Bill lingering down the hall, watching incredulously as I tell them that everything's fine. It was just a misunderstanding.

By the time I manage to struggle into pajamas, wash my face, and check the doors again, my phone lights up once more.

My chest aches. I want so badly to ignore it.

I want all of this to disappear. Crazy to think that just this morning, I was feeling so euphoric, lost to pleasure.

I tap the screen, fully expecting to see more abuse from Sal.

Instead, the text reads only: **Tomorrow night. A car will pick you up at 7 p.m. Come ready**.

The name of the contact: Last Resort.

Climbing into bed, I realize that the text doesn't make me scared or exhausted or even angry.

I'm... curious.

And maybe a bit excited.

And *maybe*... just a little bit... I feel safe.

Because if Sal is right, and Konstantin Martynov owns me, then everyone knows that he doesn't let others take what he wants.

Despite the dangers I might have to dodge, the best choice might be to give in.

To become his, entirely.

Chapter 6

Konstantin

Audrey Wolfe opens the door, and I know, without question, that I'd kill for her.

Because the first words out of my mouth are: *"Who did this to you."*

Lips parted, she steps back as I follow her into the small fourth-floor apartment. Shutting the door behind me without looking, I stalk toward her until she's backed up against a counter.

She's gorgeous.

And hurt.

And I'll kill whoever did this to her.

Bringing a hand up, I stroke the scrape that she's tried to cover with makeup. She did a good job, but I know pain when I see it. She can't disguise the swollen finger she's trying to hide behind her back or the way she winces when she moves.

"Who did this to you?"

Her eyes drop to the floor.

I grip her chin with a thumb and forefinger, raising it.

"Answer, *malen'kiy volk*."

Her brows knit at my Russian.

"My *ex*-boyfriend." There's anger in her emphasis of the "ex." Good. If he had put out her fire, I would've made his future death much more painful.

Stepping back, I consider the situation. This must be why she didn't come into work today. When I didn't see her on the screen in my office, I'd assumed she was still trying to make her mind up about tonight.

Now I can see what the real problem was.

"I'll deal with him after dinner," I murmur, rolling my shoulders. Audrey glances up at me quickly, relief in her eyes as her body loosens from the stress of whatever she went through.

Smoothing down the front of her dress, she stands on tip-toe to look over my shoulder.

"You came just... by yourself?"

"Of course not, Miss Wolfe. I have men. Around. Watching." Touching her chin lightly once more, I draw her gaze back to meet mine. "I will ask them to stay and watch *you*. Make sure he doesn't return. Besides," I say, turning and offering her my arm, "there are *some things* that I need to do personally. I have more experience than my men."

A blush darkens her cheeks as I smirk down at her. It matches her dress, sleeveless, light and layered, a floral pattern spilling down her bust and past the cream belt that gathers it all at her waist.

Good. I want her thinking of yesterday.

I want her wanting *more*.

"You look gorgeous. I wasn't sure you'd wear the dress I had delivered. I picked it out especially for you."

At the door, I take a moment to slide my fingers down her bare back. Leaning in, I whisper, "But I'm happy you obeyed."

I'm close enough to taste her lips if I want to. Audrey sways, her eyes half-lidded as I breathe in her scent. The apartment is small, cluttered lovingly in a way that makes the space between us feel incredibly small.

I could reach out and have her *now,* here, on the counter or the floor. I doubt she'd protest. Slipping my hand under the fabric, my fingers ghost over the rise of her ass, wanting to grab and knead it. Pull her closer.

"You have good taste, Mr. Martynov," Audrey whispers back, her chest rising in slow, tortured breaths. "At first I thought it might be too revealing, but..."

"Mmm, you must be referring to the low cut." I spin her abruptly, pulling her back against my body. Despite our height different, she fits perfectly against me, her ass nestled against my thighs. I let my hands ghost under her breasts, covered by narrow triangles of the dress, her cleavage beautifully on display. It's classy, tempting, promising all at once.

"You have nothing to be self-conscious of, Miss Wolfe. We should leave before I get distracted. I've worked up quite an appetite anticipating tonight."

Taking her hips firmly, I turn her again so that we're face to face. Her wounded hand is cradled between us. I take the other, reveling in the soft feel of her fingertips in my palm.

"Come."

* * *

Éclat never disappoints. The restaurant is splendid, every inch of the walls dripping in gold and elegance. It would almost be too much, except the owner, Julien Moreau, pushed it even further—to the very limits.

I watch Audrey take it in as we sit in the center of the cream-colored dining room, the gold surroundings giving her skin a glow that makes me want to reach out and touch it.

Leaning back in my chair, I let my foot trail against her leg. She jumps, winning a chuckle from me.

"Miss Wolfe. The *serveuse* is waiting."

"Oh—I apologize." Audrey turns her attention to the young woman waiting on us, whose eyes have already scrutinized her and flicked to *me*. She knows who I am, and though Moreau's staff is impeccably professional, they gossip in the back.

Which is part of why I chose this place.

"I'll have a white wine, please—"

Lips parted, Audrey glances in my direction.

"I believe I still have a bottle of Domaine Leflaive here. We'll take that."

I complete the order by choosing both plates for us, ignoring Audrey's look of contempt and then interest. With the dishes in French, and her interest in the restaurant, she hasn't had time to look closely at the menu.

The server disappears and we're left alone.

Each table is spaced far enough away to create a sense of intimacy, privacy. So, I decide to get right to business.

"Miss Wolfe—"

"Audrey."

She surprises me with the offer. And it means she's giving in, whether she knows it or not.

I smile.

"*Audrey.* I brought you here to discuss your future with my company."

A mixture of relief and disappointment crosses her pretty features.

"And as my surrogate."

Her eyes snap up to mine.

"I—you weren't kidding...?"

Leaning forward, I promise her, "I *never* kid, Miss Wolfe."

Audrey. I'll save it for later, when I'm inside her, when I'm making her come.

"And I never make a threat without promising through. You took something of mine; you owe me something in return. And I want a child."

Her face turns red as she glances quickly around the room, trying to figure out if anyone has heard my declaration.

"I've already had my lawyers draft up an agreement." I place the folder on the table. "It's simple: you'll act as a surrogate under my care. You'll carry my child to term, and birth him or her. Once the child—and you—are healthy, you are out of my debt."

Audrey stares at me, her fingers wrapped around the stem of the wine glass that the server just brought.

"You can't be serious, Mr. Martynov."

"Call me Konstantin."

She scoffs, looking down at the table. "You... you want

me to get pregnant. Why me? You don't know anything about me, or my family or genetics, or..."

I watch the realization take over her face as she remembers exactly *who I am.* Of course, I know all about her. I looked into her the very day I saw her on the construction site, in that mobile office.

"Come here."

Her brows knit, and I gesture at the space beside me. When she doesn't move, I growl again: *"Come here."*

Audrey flinches, then stands, clearly embarrassed at drawing attention. A few other guests are watching passively. They know better than to show too much interest in my affairs. Audrey awkwardly moves the elegant chair to my side, and slips her curves into it once more, putting her within reach.

I lean over casually, a hand on her thigh. My fingers slowly work the fabric up her lower half as I explain: "I know enough. I know all that I need to know. And I've chosen you. So, your options are, either agree... or take a different kind of punishment. You'll find, Audrey, that being close to me can be very... pleasurable."

My fingers touch skin, and I slide my hand between her thighs, grazing her center. Her silk panties are already damp. "Good girl," I murmur, feeling the throb of heat at the praise.

She licks her lips.

"I can bring you pleasure, but I can also bring you pain. It's your choice."

Sitting back, I pull my fingers away. She lets out a small gasp and clamps her legs shut tightly. The server arrives with our food—blanquette de veau for myself, sole menuière for her—and Audrey's lips are pursed until she leaves.

When she speaks, her questions are direct, logical... and I know I have her in my snare.

She won't say no.

She can't.

"So, how exactly would we do this Mr. Martynov? Artificial insemination I'm assuming?"

I cut her off with a shake of my head. "No, no, *malen'kiy volk*. I'm a man who likes to do things the *right* way. To do them myself."

My eyes drag down her body, what's visible next to me: her curves tight against the dress, the swell of her breasts in the low-cut bodice, her ass filling the seat.

"You... you mean..."

I dip a finger into the veal sauce and raise it to her mouth. "Try it."

She's caught off guard, looking first at my eyes and then at the offering. Once again, she proves that she's capable of obeying me, even with hate in her gaze.

Audrey leans forward, opens her mouth, and lets my finger ghost over her lips. She delights me by flicking her tongue out to taste the creamy sauce.

"I mean," I whisper, leaning in and making a show of moving her hair behind her ear with my other hand, "that I plan to take you to bed, tease you until you're begging, fill you with my seed, and hold those pretty little thighs of yours shut until it takes."

When I pull away, her eyes are hazy with lust and confusion.

"Eat, Miss Wolfe. You can look over the contract tonight."

My tone brooks no argument; she gives me one more glance before picking up her fork and lifting a piece of flaky, delicate fish to her lips.

Now that I know what they feel like wrapped around my finger, I'm determined to feel them wrapped around something *else*.

My little wolf is back.

She's silent on the car ride to her apartment, noticing the car tailing us with two of my soldiers, and likely the car pulling away from her apartment building—making sure it's safe for her to enter.

Before I can open her door, Audrey does it herself and stumbles out, not careful enough on her still-bruised ankle. She attempts to walk right by me without a single look.

I reach out and catch her wrist, holding firm.

"Not even a thank you."

She stands on the sidewalk, trying not to let her fear show. But I can see it just under her skin as my eyes trail down her taut body once more.

"Thank you," she cuts out, "but I don't think I'm interested in this arrangement. I'll find a way to pay you back."

I laugh.

"Whether or not you can return the money, it's not what I want."

Stepping forward, I close the space between us, jerking

Audrey against my body. The streetlights spill across her skin, making it look warm and inviting.

"I'm tempted to take you upstairs and desecrate your little apartment. Show you exactly what I want. You think I don't know how wet you were earlier, when I touched you under the table? Imagine what I can do to you when we're alone."

She pulls away.

I let her go. It might be what's needed to make her feel like she has control, an option, even if she doesn't. If she says no, I'll hunt her down and take her. But I'd prefer her to come willingly.

"I'm not interested," she chokes out half-way to the door, fumbling for her keys.

"It doesn't matter if you're interested," I call after her. "Everyone in the city knows you're mine, Miss Wolfe, after tonight. They'll be coming after you one way or another. If you want protection—if you want to stay alive—you'll come to me."

Chapter 7

Audrey

"Please state your reason for missing your shift today."

The voice on the other end of the call could almost be a recording. My face heats as I lie, again: "Illness."

This is the second day in a row I've called in sick, needing time to think after the volatile and... frustratingly tempting evening I spent with Mr. Martynov.

Or Konstantin, as he asked me to call him, but that feels forbidden. Like I'm tempting fate if I utter his given name.

"Thank you. Please be aware that eight hours will be removed from your current PTO cache, which stands at four-hundred-and-sixteen hours as of this call."

A *click* on the other end signifies that the call is ended. It's very Martynov Global Holdings: cold, direct, succinct.

I put my phone face-down on the counter and, wrapping the wool blanket tighter around my shoulders, head back to the couch. I almost *feel* actually sick with how nervous I've been since that night.

Mr. Martynov's—Konstantin's—words ring in my head: *Everyone in the city knows you're mine.*

They'll be coming after you one way or another.

The curtains are drawn over my windows, but amber, dawn light still spills in. Knees to my chest on the couch, I try to push away the ache of tears coming on. But one glance at Nana's photo on the shelf makes them spill over.

"What do I do?" I whisper to her.

I've always wanted a kid. Or *kids,* I'd once imagined— what seems like forever ago, when I was fresh into my first year of college and dreaming of my future. My degree first, and maybe I'd fall in love with some handsome guy from class, and we'd get engaged, and have a small but tasteful wedding. Nana would have walked me down the aisle. Kids a year or so later. We'd be happy.

Instead, here I am.

Wrapped up on the couch, shaking at the thought of —what?

Of Konstantin Martynov owning me?

Of owing him tens of thousands of dollars?

The morning drags by, and I manage to fall into a lull after a night of not sleeping well. Drifting off, head literally nodding, I'm brought back by the buzz of my phone.

It's Chrissy: **You alright? Out again today?**

Yeah, I type back, guilt making me answer quickly. **Can you talk sometime today? Maybe stop by later?**

I imagine what the office is like: Chrissy, Jeannette, Grace, and Duscha will all be settling in. The printers humming; computers blinking on. The guys from Operations, in their dark suits with multiple phones hidden in their pockets, already whispering in other languages as they check in on their territories.

And Konstantin…

Sprawled out in that chair, in his office, where he bent me over the desk. Where he knelt in front of me and almost had me begging.

If I do this, agree to his terms, it releases me from my debt.

If I do this I'm safe. From Sal, at least—who's to say how long Konstantin will put up with my fresh mouth?

Or what he'll do with it once I give him the reins?

Taking a deep breath, I confirm with Chrissy that she can swing by for lunch and drop off soup from our favorite café. Then, I dial another number cryptically saved in my phone under Black Echo.

It rings once, and then a voice answers, cold, calculated. "Operator."

"My name is Audrey Wolfe, Head Accountant Number 5. Please connect me to Marty." It's an inside joke, because the last thing Konstantin is, is a martyr.

This is the test.

If Konstantin is serious about his offer, I'll be transferred through—to his direct line. As far as I know, no one has access to his direct line except for his seconds-in-command.

"One moment."

There's a click, and the line goes silent for so long that I think they've hung up. A flush of embarrassment erupts on my cheeks, hot and tingling, making me hide my face in the blanket.

I'm just about to hang up when the line clicks again.

There's breathing on the other end; slow, steady, like a predator waiting in a dark cave.

And I'm the prey willingly walking into the shadows.

"Konstantin?"

"*Malen'kiy volk.*"

My nose scrunches, but now isn't the time to ask what the strange nickname means. I could just google it, but I'm half-afraid to.

"I... I've thought about your offer. I have some terms of my own."

There's a harsh laugh, different from the throaty, sexy chuckle he's let loose a few times—only when he has me mindless, knees spread.

This laugh reminds me of who he really is, a murderer who killed his way to the top of the ladder. Who has no problem being drenched in blood or wearing a perfectly tailored suit.

When he doesn't speak, I swallow and continue: "I'll be your surrogate. And I... understand your preference for how we... go about the task." That earns me an appreciative hum, one I imagine him making between my legs someday. I squirm on the couch, trying to focus.

This is life or death. For me, at least.

"Marriage is off the table."

The silence echoes. I've caught him off guard.

Then I feel like an idiot, though, because why would it have ever been *on* the table?

Why would a man like Konstantin Martynov want a woman like *me*?

"And when the baby is born, once I've recovered, I want

a one-way ticket to the west coast. First class. And I want you to pay for whatever I need to settle there."

My heart aches at the thought of leaving New York, but I just can't stay. Especially if the plan is for me to carry a child to term, and then... walk away from it.

I can't just do it metaphorically. A small, sad part of me knows that no matter how I go about this, even understanding that it's a business transaction, there's the danger of getting attached.

"You would leave your child."

Konstantin's voice is cold, a different kind of cold than I've heard before. It makes me shiver with shame. This could change his mind, a woman so heartless carrying his child.

"Yes," I answer, unhesitating. "It's a second chance for me, just as it's a legacy for you. You'll get what you want. I'll get safety. You pointed out last night—they know I'm yours now," the words send a thrill of fear through me. "They'll come after me, even if I don't mean anything to you. Leaving is the only way I'll be safe."

I don't say the other reason I'm seeking safety: Sal.

He promised to come after me and take me down with Konstantin. I don't know exactly what his plans are. As far as I can tell, he's low on the totem pole when it comes to the Italian mafia. He was my accidental in, my bankroll when I needed that money to pay for Nana. And he could be my demise, if I don't get out of here.

"Where are you."

The change in conversation surprises me enough that I look around the small apartment. I remember him here two nights ago—his towering form just inside my doorway, the glint of streetlights on his silver hair. *Never* would I have imagined I'd see a man as elegant and threatening as Konstantin Martynov in my home.

"I'm home today. Sick," I lie, knowing he catches the fib as soon as he lets out a chuckle.

That low, dark sound that goes right to my core. I squeeze my legs together, eyes closed as I try to bring back the sensation of his big hand on my thigh, his fingers delving down.

"You're missing another day."

"I... yes."

"If your accounts are behind, Miss Wolfe, I'll have to punish you."

There it is again: the threat to punish me.

I bite my tongue, tempted to call his bluff. Tempted to fudge some of the numbers if it gets me in his hands again.

"I had to think things over."

"Mmm. And did you think about me, Audrey?"

The question could be harmless, but it's not; I feel it in the thrum of his voice. Restless, I'm not sure how to answer, because the truth is I *have* thought of him. I've relived the night I sent him that text a few times, the way he leaned me over in his office the next day, the sound of his belt coming off.

My pussy pulses, mind going blank at the instinctual need.

"Be outside of your apartment in twenty minutes."

I sit up straight, almost dropping the blanket. "What?"

"You have twenty minutes. Get dressed. But don't you dare put panties on, Audrey."

The pulse turns to a throb of *want*. I fight it. He might

own me for however long it takes for him to fuck me preg-nant, but I refuse to let him control every aspect of my life.

"I have plans for lunch—"

"Cancel them. You're mine. I'm going to make you feel it."

My mouth snaps shut.

No matter how badly I want to protest, I know I'll obey.

Chapter 8

Konstantin

It's a breezy autumn day, crisp and alive with the leaves chattering in the trees. Audrey is standing under a streetlight when I get out of the car.

The wind lifts her skirt, and she palms it down quickly, a blush on her cheeks.

Good. That means she did what I told her to do.

The thought that she's standing there without panties on, waiting for me, the cool air playing over her flesh... it's all I can do not to pick her up, carry her up to her little apartment, and fuck her until she's screaming my name.

Instead, I get close—so close I can feel the heat of her body, smell the scent of her freshly washed hair—and slip a cell phone into her hand.

"This is yours."

She turns it over in her palm, looking at it quizzically. "Um, thank you, but I already have a phone—"

Grabbing her wrist with one hand, I deftly tap the screen with the other. Her pulse races under my thumb. I pull the contacts up. There's only one entry.

"This is my personal number. Not through the operator, not through the emergency line—*my* number."

Audrey looks up at me with wide eyes, comprehension dawning.

"It will be the only number in this phone. Do you understand?"

She nods, fingers closing around the brand new, sleek phone as she holds it tightly to her chest.

Turning, I start for the Alfa Romeo. Audrey takes a hesitant step behind me.

"Konstantin?"

The sound of my name on her lips sends a tremor through my muscles, like a small earthquake. I'm momentarily caught off guard by just how easily this woman can unground me. I've fought men with my bare hands, killed with knives and guns, woken from a coma, survived starving on the streets.

And I'd do it all again to fall at her feet.

The feeling is overwhelming, and I can't let her see it—how much control she has *just by saying my name.*

So, I wait.

She bites her lip in the silence, then asks, "Where are we going?"

"You'll see. Get in the car."

* * *

Twenty minutes later, thanks to a lack of traffic, I park the purring car outside of a newly-built house. I chose it myself out of our catalog, holding back from buying her the biggest and most ostentatious house I could offer.

I don't know Audrey well—yet—but I can tell by her style that more isn't necessarily better, for her. Just that one evening in her apartment, even with my focus on her pain and fear, I gathered enough to know that she likes comfort.

Closeness.

Two cars pull up down the street behind us. I don't need to explain to Audrey who they are; the men watch as I get out of the Alfa. Two follow, standing a respectable distance away in the cover of Japanese maples.

The house is a 1930s style country cape, painted slate blue with white accents. The transom door is arched, the windows large and diamond paned, looking out onto a yard that I paid an abhorrent amount to make look lush and old-growth.

When Audrey takes my hand and steps out of the car, it's easy to see that she already loves it.

Her features shift from amazement to excitement and then, unexpectedly, disappointment.

"You don't like it?"

Her pretty eyes flick my way, then take in the little yard, the rock driveway, the hidden turret on the side of the house where I imagine she'll soak in sunlight while growing our child. Protected; hidden; happy.

"No, I... I love it. It's beautiful."

Taking her hand, I practically drag her up the walkway and to the door. The men follow, still at a distance. The key is styled to look antique, but there's a lock pad too, an extra measure of security. Aside from the countless cameras on the property and the high-end alarm system that the team installed yesterday morning.

I knew she'd say yes.

Even before that call this morning.

"Then why do you have that look on your face?" I ask her once we step inside, tipping her chin upward, studying her thick lashes and full lips. They're as enticing as her curves as I ghost my hand over her hips.

But there will be time for that later. Right now, eyes narrowed, I need to know why she looks so forlorn.

There's a flash of fear in her eyes. Her lips purse: a tell-tale sign that she doesn't want to admit to something.

"Audrey," I murmur in a low warning, pulling her close by her wrist. "I will only say this once: You *do not* want to lie to me. When I ask you a question, I expect the truth. Answer me."

Her eyes dart away. They sweep across the furnishings, perfectly curated to fit the home: a narrow console table with a vase of out-of-season hydrangeas, an ornate coat rack, beautiful oak detailing around the door interior.

"It's gorgeous. It's exactly what I'd want for myself, but it's not mine, is it?"

Pressing the key into her palm, I answer, "It is. This is your home, Audrey."

Her laugh is throaty, but there's hurt in it too. "Not really though Konstantin. Nothing is mine that I don't earn. I didn't earn this."

Gripping her hips tightly, I lean in, tempted to steal a kiss right here.

"Oh, but you will earn it, Audrey. If you really want it, you'll *earn* it."

A flush crawls prettily up her neck from the bow tied at her throat. Reaching up, I pull one end and watch it unravel, exposing her collarbones. When I lean in I can smell her scent: that vanilla citrus, a warmth that draws me like a moth to a flame.

"As long as you carry our child, this will be your home. This is where you'll be safe."

When I pull away, there's a different look in her eyes. Feverish and bright. She searches my face, swaying forward unsteadily, and I think for a moment that *she* might be the one who steals a kiss.

Then she steps back, looking shyly down.

"Can I see the rest?"

With a gesture, I release her. Audrey is tentative at first, then more exploratory as she roams the little halls. The kitchen, then the living room, and entrance to the turret room. On the other side of the house, a dining area and a wood-paneled, walk-in pantry.

I follow her upstairs, tempted to reach out and grip the backs of her thighs with my hands. To cup her ass, take her there on the stairs; the way her skirt bounces with each step is a tease, especially knowing that were I to reach under, find my way up her inner thigh, there'd be nothing to stop me from stroking her warm, needy pussy.

Barefoot since the foyer, Audrey wanders into a full bathroom with a clawfoot tub, the second floor of the turret room—with a seating area that looks down to the first floor, letting light spill in from the wall of windows—and two bedrooms. One is minimally furnished. I don't want her inviting just anyone to this house, but I'll explain that later. Or Lev can. I have other things to take care of first.

She passes a window, nearing the master bedroom. Pausing, I gesture to the men outside. They confer, then move back toward their cars.

"Tell me," I murmur, following her into the bedroom. "Did you follow my instructions?"

She stands on a plush carpet, toes sinking into it, looking vulnerable in the dying light and the large room. The bed is a king, doused in elegant beige and blue bedding with antique rose patterns.

Audrey's hands fist in her skirt.

I stalk toward her, satisfied at the sight of the undone bow at her neck, her tousled hair, the flush on her cheeks.

"Show me."

She licks her lips, moving to take a step forward.

"No. Pull your skirt up. Slowly. And show me that pretty pussy, *malen'kiy volk.*"

The heavy, luxurious fabric rises as she inches it up her legs. She gets to mid-thigh and my mouth waters at the sight that I've only fantasized about. Already my cock is throbbing with interest.

There.

That's mine.

I've had her in my office, lapping at her folds, but in the golden light spilling through the window I can see every inch of her. She's wet, pink, and inviting.

"Stay like that," I command.

Audrey obeys. She's straining to breathe, to get a rhythm as I move toward her, shoes echoing on the hardwood floor. I kick them off at the edge of the carpet and circle her, slowly, taking in her thick legs and round, exposed ass.

When I come near, she makes a sound close to a whimper and a gasp. My hands rest on her hips, then slip forward, slowly, caressing.

"Please," she whispers.

My fingers hover over her heat. It's taking everything in me to hold back, to tease her like this.

"What do you want, little wolf?"

Audrey leans back, her ass tucked up against me, making my dick throb more insistently. It wants out; it wants to claim what's ours.

"I... I want you to touch me. Please."

"Say my name."

I'm almost ashamed to ask it of her, but I put force behind the words. I want to feel control. I want her to obey. And I want to make sure she knows just who is making her tremble tonight.

"Please touch me, Konstantin." It comes out as a breathy request, and I can't hold back anymore. Burying my face in her neck, sucking and biting the delicate skin there, I delve two fingers into her slick and come back to circle her clit.

She's taut as a bow string, back arching and hands clenched in the skirt as she holds it up and lets me ruin her.

"Like this?" I ask, plunging into her entrance so abruptly that she cries out. "Is this what you want?"

Audrey whines, trying to find purchase on the carpet as she instinctually bends at the hips, pressing herself back on my erection. I grip her hip with my free hand, grinding against her ass.

It doesn't take much to bring her to the edge but, like that day in the office, I don't let her come. Instead, I spin her around, the surprise of the movement making her drop her skirt.

"Take it off."

She quickly undoes the zipper, stumbling as I stalk toward her, guiding her to the bed.

This, all this, is for her.

And tonight, I'll finally claim her as mine.

I'll fuck her into this bed until she's carrying my child.

"This, too," I murmur, grazing the undone tie of the bow. There's barely any space between us. Audrey crosses her arms, lifts the bottom of the shirt, and it slides off, mussing her hair even more.

She's in nothing but a bra.

"How do you want to...?" she asks breathlessly, her eyes dragging down to my trousers, where my arousal is apparent. "I can turn around, or help you get close, or..."

"No."

Holding her by the hips, I push her onto the bed, hefting her voluptuous body further up and spreading her knees apart.

"You're already wet."

She inhales sharply at the satisfied grin on my face.

"I want you to stay just like this. And wait for me."

Slowly, I undo my shirt button by button, shucking it off. The undershirt beneath is clean, white, and tucked into my trousers. Audrey licks her lips at the sound of my belt coming undone, and I know she's thinking of that day in my office. I've been thinking of it, too.

"This isn't going to be clinical," I warn. "I'm not going to be gentle with you."

Audrey nods, gripping the thick duvet, knees still spread and pussy still glistening. I take my time, removing my trousers and folding them, laying them on the bed. Doing the same with my boxers.

Letting her get an eyeful of just how badly I want her.

I'm already rock hard when I kneel on the bed with one knee, fisting myself and dragging a slow, teasing stroke to the tip. A bead of precum leaks out and Audrey sits up on her elbows, eyes locked on to my cock.

"Are we alone?" she asks nervously, eyes darting to the open door.

I grab her ankle, dragging her toward me, and she lets out a surprised yelp.

"We are. But it doesn't matter. They'll hear you screaming for me from the cars."

Holding her hips down with one hand, I guide my cock to her clit, dragging over it slowly. Over and over. Until she's twitching under me, a damp spot on the duvet.

I can tell she's resisting the pleasure by how she bites her lip. *I'll break her.* I'll have her begging for me.

"Don't move," I tell her, holding her thighs as far apart as possible and lining myself up at her entrance. I watch my cock press into her, stretching her swollen pussy, filling her the way I've always imagined. Audrey lets out a whimper, her hips shifting.

"Don't move."

Stopping midway, I reach up her body, wrapping my hand around her throat. Audrey tips her head back obediently. "You don't move until I tell you to, understand? You're going to wait while I fuck you, you're going to wait until I tell you that you can come all over my cock."

Adjusting her roughly, I try to ignore the abrupt throb of pleasure as I slide deeper into her. Audrey lets out a low moan, throwing her head back, legs spread wide for me.

"Good girl."

My hips crash into hers, brutally, the sound of slapping flesh obscene in the pristine room. Pulling back, her pussy makes a sucking noise, and I plunge in again, burying myself deep. Holding her against me hard, fucking into her over and over.

Slow.

Deliberate.

"You're mine."

She's panting under me, body trembling with the effort of staying still as I fuck her.

"Say it, *malen'kiy volk.*"

"I—I'm yours!"

"Say my name."

"Konstantin. I'm yours Konstantin."

As a reward, I graze my thumb over her clit. I can feel myself getting closer, getting lost in the warm, sopping sensation of her pussy surrounding me. Audrey's hips jerk. She can't help it, but I give her ass a light slap as a reminder of who is in charge.

Her moans get higher in pitch. She's close, so I bury myself in her and fuck her quickly, shallow, feeling my cock bottom out as her hips match my rhythm. Putting my other knee on the bed, I lean over her, fingers still playing her clit.

"You'll tell me," I grunt, fucking her harder. "I know you've been lying to me, Audrey, and I'll find out the truth. You'll tell me who put you up to stealing the money. You'll tell me why. And then you'll let me fuck you like this, over and over, because *you're mine.*"

Her pussy clenches around me as she orgasms, a shudder going through her whole body. Finally, I lose myself in the sensation of her taking me, every inch of me. I

71

know she'll be bruised and sore later, and it makes this even more delicious.

As her hips twitch under me, I give in to the ever-tightening heat and fill her with my seed. Slowing, I fuck into her over and over. Making sure to bury it deep. To give her every last drop.

To begin my legacy with her beneath me.

Chapter 9

Audrey

I t's like waking up on a cloud.

That's all I can think as I burrow deeper into the duvet, the scent unrecognizable; definitely not the bed in my apartment...

Then it comes back in a rush. Especially when my pussy throbs, making me draw my knees up.

I open my eyes and peer out from the pile of luxurious bedding. Cream, blue, white; the room is beautiful. The windows are tall, letting morning light spill in, and the furniture is simple but gives off an air of elegance.

My heart aches with how much I love every detail.

How did he know?

Konstantin.

Feeling the stickiness between my thighs, I sit up with a blush, expecting--what?

I'm alone.

Of course he's not here; he's Konstantin Martynov.

The blush turns into a flush of embarrassment. Would a

man like him ever actually spend the night in bed with a woman like me? Wake next to me, so I don't feel so... alone?

With a shiver, I remember that as much as I love the décor, I don't actually know this house. I barely remember the layout, and that makes me feel vulnerable, so I slip out of the bed quickly.

There's a trickle of warmth down my thigh. Ignoring thoughts of the previous night—of how easily I gave in to him—I pad over to the ensuite and refuse to look in the mirror, searching out hand towels and running warm water.

Should I... clean up here? Take a bath? It's tempting; the clawfoot tub is beautiful, and I wouldn't mind soaking. The last two weeks, the stress, have left me tense and on edge.

Last night was the first time I felt any kind of release.

Any kind of mindless pleasure, giving in entirely to someone else's control.

Oh, God. The way I just let him do whatever he wanted to me.

Okay, I need to be realistic about this. Glancing out the window, it's obviously well past morning. The neighborhood is quiet; I can barely see the next house over through the oak trees, and there's a sense of privacy here.

How the hell am I going to get home?

I'm not even sure which direction the city is in, although I'm sure once I clear the trees I'll be able to see the buildings. Craning, I try to see if the cars are still parked down the street—after all, he's been having men watching me. He made that very clear.

He wouldn't leave me all alone in this house, right? With no security, no protection?

Especially considering I might already be conceiving his child.

* * *

Fifteen minutes later I'm relatively cleaned up, and trying to decide if I should call a cab company, an Uber, or just wait until he calls.

Two cell phones sit on the bedside table. My old, scratched up phone and the gleaming new one he gave me the night before.

Should I text him? Surely he'll be at the Spire by now. Shouldn't *I* be there too, now that I've missed several days of work?

Anxiety makes me feel itchy, restless, and I jump when there's a light knock on the doorframe.

"Miss Wolfe."

A pretty older woman stands there, dressed in what is clearly a starched work uniform. There are several bags next to me that look out of place in the butter-colored hallway.

Because they're *my* bags.

A beat-up duffle bag with a loud, ochre-and-blue pattern and several suitcases I found in thrift stores: worn leather in varying stages of falling apart, teals and browns and a dark red.

"Mr. Martynov had your things packed and brought here. At least, for a few days, until you move in. There is a company waiting for your call today whenever you would like to do so. Can I make you breakfast?"

She looks at me inquiringly, as if it's totally normal for a mafia boss to buy a house, furnish it, hire staff, fuck his mistress in it, and then... what? Expect her to live here?

"Sorry, he... wants me to move in?"

Her eyes narrow briefly, quickly. "Did he not clarify that last night, when he showed you the house?"

Oh, he did more than show me the house, but she can already guess that from the rumpled state of my clothes and the bed.

His words from the night before swim back to my memory: *This is your home, Audrey.*

The key.

It sits on the nightstand, beautifully intricate and heavy. *You'll earn it.*

My core throbs with the memory, and the promise of just what I'd have to do to *earn it.* Ugh, I shouldn't be so turned on by this arrangement.

After all, I'm letting my boss fuck me until I'm pregnant. I'm *enjoying my mafia, murdering boss fucking me until I'm pregnant with his child.*

It's all too much, and my eyes well with tears. The woman, whose name I don't know, takes a gentle step back.

"I'll give you some privacy, miss. When you're ready, I'll be downstairs."

She disappears, leaving my bags just outside the door and the start of tears rolling down my cheeks.

What the hell have I gotten myself into?

* * *

When I finally pad downstairs, everything is like a dream.

There are vases of flowers—hydrangeas, baby's breath,

bluebells, something pink and layered I don't recognize—on almost every surface.

"Those are camellias."

Startled, I turn to find the woman watching me from the open archway that leads to the kitchen. She nods to the pink flowers that look more like small shrubs, thick and hearty.

"They symbolize longing," she adds with a knowing glance before disappearing into the kitchen.

I follow. It's homey, not too big, not too small. There's a long butcher block island with seats on one side and windows that look out onto the wooded yard, now draped in gold and red for the fall.

"Um, I'm Audrey," I introduce myself. "Do you work here... all the time?"

She hides a small smile, cracking eggs into a bowl. "Yes. I used to work for Mr. Martynov at another home, but he asked me to move here instead, full-time. My name is Kashmere. What would you like in your omlette, Miss Audrey?"

"Oh, um, anything is fine. Tomatoes? Cheese?" I shrug and she laughs, turning on the gas stove. "Do you mind?" I ask after a few moments, sliding into one of the island chairs. "Working here, I mean. I'm sorry if it was a surprise."

Kashmere shakes her head. "No, it wasn't, he asked me about two weeks ago now."

Two... weeks?

But he only proposed this *arrangement* last week.

I only *agreed* yesterday!

My mouth falls open in disbelief, but I don't know whether to be angry or confused. Surely he couldn't have planned all this...

No.

Ignoring my frustration, I get up and wander around the kitchen, peering into the living area and then strolling back toward the refrigerator.

Inside is an assortment of things I love strawberries, *real ones,* not perfectly shaped and huge but small and dark red; hazelnut creamer; a stash of brie; butter lettuce and full drawers that I don't open, surprised.

It's unnerving, and I'm not sure how to react. Everything is so *perfect.* I sit down and try to chat with Kashmere as she cooks, asking about her family, where she lives, and what she does when she's not at work. I'm happy to find we both love reading and promise to trade books with her.

Once I have mine moved here.

As I eat Kashmere excuses herself; she needs to pick up the last of the linens from the dry cleaner and stop at the store.

I wash the dishes slowly, watching the soapy water slip down the drain. This is all so... strange. Just last night, Konstantin brought me here and made me his.

It was visceral, electric, layered. I haven't been fucked like that *ever,* and it scares me how much I liked it.

"Maybe I'm actually crazy," I whisper, making my way back upstairs to continue exploring. "Maybe he did punish me, and I'm in a coma somewhere, fantasizing all this."

Because there's no way Konstantin Martynov would pick *me.* Especially after I stole from him.

In the master bathroom, once again I find all of my essentials. Down to the very hairbrush I like to use, so I guess I won't have to bother getting that from the apartment.

There's a blue, orange, and white tube of hand cream on

the counter and I pick it up, feeling both overwhelmed and deeply seen. It's my *favorite,* something I order directly from Italy at an absurd cost: Santa Maria Novella.

Popping the cap open, I squeeze a little in my palms and revel in the lemon scent as it opens up my senses.

And then I hear the click of heels.

"So," Olena Belov, Konstantin's right hand "man", stands in the doorway with narrowed eyes. "*This* is what has had him so preoccupied."

Chapter 10

Konstantin

O lena walks across the construction site like an angel of death.

The men stop what they're doing in her wake, but none of them dare look at her.

There are many rumors about Olena Belov.

That she killed a man in Prague with a sugar spoon.

That she was trained by the Spetsnaz, the special forces, but was abused—and took her pound of flesh for it.

That she burned down a safehouse from the inside, and walked out of the smoke once the flames died out.

That she broke a man's spine so precisely, he lived for two more days, convinced that she would come for him at any moment.

I'm the only one who knows whether or not there is truth to any of these rumors. And I'll never tell. If anyone in my organization has a chance against me—it's her.

Her head is shaved, brows so pale they seem nonexistent, and her blue eyes are striking against porcelain skin. Her strange, ethereal features stand out all the more against the all-black ensemble she insists on wearing. She moves purposefully across the littered ground despite the stilettos she wears.

Putting the sledgehammer head-down, I lean on the handle and wait for my sentence.

"Konstantin."

"Olena. I'm surprised to see you here."

Her eyes scan the site. It's a mess, and it smells like trash and the wet water of the sound. But in nine months there'll be forty-two condos. Mid-level, mid-income, and empty—unless someone is in need of a safehouse.

"There," I gesture, toward a roughed-out concrete pad. "That will be the main office. Passports and papers. And the laundry rooms—" another, much smaller, concrete pad with the makings of an electric line, "for laundering, of course."

Olena tries to look interested, but she's distracted.

Which means she's found out.

She's found *her*.

"Can we talk? Preferably somewhere with four walls enclosing us?"

The men know better than to murmur, but they're beginning to cluster. They've become so used to me visiting the sites, throwing on a high-vis vest, and shoveling or sawing or destroying. It's interesting that a visit from Olena is what sets them on edge.

"Rein's. Let's go."

Rein's Deli is as packed as always. It smells of pastrami, pickles, and diner coffee. Olena gets less glances here than at the construction site; I blend in perfectly in work pants and a sweat-stained shirt.

"Mr. Martynov," greets the chef.

"Spencer. Your boss around?"

"No, not today, sir. He's at his daughter's basketball game. I can call him—"

"No, no. I just wanted to check that the issue with the health department was taken care of."

"It was sir. Thank you. Your usual?"

"Yes, please. And whatever Olena would like."

Olena browses the menu, making an impossibly quick decision: "Kippered salmon salad and stuffed cabbage."

Spencer nods and gets to work, calling the order out to his prep and sous chefs.

We settle into a booth, Olena's long legs stretched to the side, ankles crossed.

"What exactly are you doing?" The question is mild, but direct.

"I am starting a family," I tell her. "A legacy."

She snorts. "A family? Does that seem like a good idea to you, Konstantin, considering where you came from?"

My brother Mikhail's face flashes through my mind; the look he gave me the day I left.

The fact that I never saw him when I returned.

"I know it's hard to believe, Olena, but it doesn't have to be like that."

Her features harden. The coffee arrives and the conversation goes quiet until the server steps away respectfully.

One thing I don't know about Olena is her family situation. I've heard talk that she was an orphan, that her uncle traded her for drugs, that she still has sisters somewhere.

She's never chosen to share that information with me, and I will never pry. Having Olena on my side is safer than having her as an enemy.

"Have you thought about how vulnerable this will make you? Having a wife—"

"I don't intend to marry her."

Her smirk is slow, making my stomach clench in annoyance.

"Oh, so you're just using her? Isn't she a bit young for you, Konstantin?"

"She's a surrogate. She'll give me a child, and then we have an agreement. She'll leave New York."

"Mmm. Do you know many men who house their surrogates in expensive houses? Who assign entire teams of men to watch after them, keep them safe?"

I put the coffee cup down with a loud crack. Olena doesn't flinch, but she taps her nails on the tabletop, a sign that she senses how on edge I am.

"What would you have me do, Olena? Who will take over for me? I'm old already, almost fifty, and I have no legacy. Can you name someone else in the group who should succeed me?"

She bites her tongue as our food arrives.

There is *no one*. We both know that.

Should she suggest herself, I'd be open to it. But Olena wants to lead Martynov Global Holdings as much as she wants to saw out her own spleen. Olena is a raven; smart, resourceful, too clever to get stuck in a corner. She wants an out, always.

"There are other things you should be worrying about, Konstantin. Like Giuseppe Sartorre."

That gets my attention. "What about Sartorre? He's minding his business, staying on his side of the city."

"Is he?"

The casual lilt to her words makes me freeze.

Have I missed something, in my haze of desire these past few months? Has something—or someone—slipped through the cracks?

"Tell me."

Olena leans back, picking at the flaked salmon and rye bread. "Two men were killed at the Lux last week. Two of ours. We have reason to believe it was Sartorre, or at least men working for him."

"What reason?"

"The camera shows one of them with a tattoo of a compass pointing north on his forearm."

The Northern Line.

Giuseppe Sartorre's gang. Though "gang" makes them sound trivial. He's an offshoot of the Italian mob, controlling a large portion of the northern part of the city.

And it sounds like his men have weaseled their way into my territory.

"Why wasn't I told about this?"

"When should we have told you? While you were fucking her in your office, or picking out paint for the house?"

I snarl across the table, ignoring the Reuben in front of me. "I wasn't fucking her in my office. I should have been told. I should come down on you, Olena, for not making sure I was told."

She stares at me, waiting—for punishment or mercy. I

know what I should do, but Olena is the closest thing to family I have. She's a weak spot.

Someday she might kill me, and I might let her. The sister I never had.

Mikhail's face flashes through my mind again. And then my mother, screaming in Russian: *Go then! Get out of here, you rat! You've been living off my teat for long enough!*

Ironic, since as soon as I began making money in America, it was *she* who lived off *me*.

"A child won't fix things," Olena says as if reading my mind. "Only create complications."

"I have things under control. Audrey Wolfe will give me a child, and he or she will be raised within the empire, Olena. Their life will be different than mine—than *ours* was. And someday, they will lead."

She doesn't look convinced. But my tone brooks no argument. Still, I feel compelled to give her something. To justify my obsession with Audrey.

"Someone used her to get into my accounts, Olena. If you're truly concerned about Giuseppe Sartorre, let me get what I can out of her. She may be the key to why he's snooping around our territory. I just need to break her."

"I hope you're right, Konstantin. If you aren't..."

She doesn't need to finish that sentence.

If I'm wrong, Audrey Wolfe could be the death of me.

If I'm not, I could have it all—everything I want.

Her.

A child.

Complete control over my future, my territory, my story.

I won't go into that final night the ragged boy that was

spit out of Russia. I won't be the weak, good-for-nothing man that my mother insisted I was.

No; I've made it this far.

I have everything.

But I want more. And I'll take what I want. Destroying whoever stands in my way.

Chapter 11

Audrey

The library at 7 a.m. is empty aside from the workers, and I hurry down the hallway to the main desk that sprawls across the first level.

Emil stands before a small pile of books, cataloging the new arrivals with gloved hands. They will go into the archives, a climate-controlled room, to be accessed by those who will respect and worship them.

"Audrey! Are you okay? I was starting to get worried."

He looks, somehow, even older since the last time I saw him—only weeks ago.

"Yes, I'm sorry Emil. I'm fine. It's just been so busy—at work." I try to fight down the heat of the lie, even though it isn't *completely* a lie. Today, Thursday, is my first day back after several days off. After settling into the house that my boss purchased for me.

Which will be mine, if I carry his child.

My stomach twists with nerves. It has to be just nerves, right? Surely it's too early to actually be pregnant, to *feel* anything...

Emil's eyes, young and sharp despite his age, narrow. "You're sure you've been alright?" When I give him a flat look, he apologizes: "You know your grandmother would never forgive me if I didn't look out for you, Audrey."

His smile is sad, but in it I see just how much he loved Nana. In secret, or... maybe not. It was obvious to everyone but her that Emil was infatuated with her. When she got sick, he was there almost every day, reading to her or bringing by boxes of protein shakes. Filling the living room with her favorite flowers and playing music, they used to dance to when she was healthy.

"I know," I murmur, reaching out to touch his wrinkled hand. "Thank you. I really am fine, Emil, I've just been overwhelmed lately. I promise I'll stop by more often. Do you have...?"

With a sigh, he ambles off to find the stack of books that I requested about a month ago. I trade him another, finished stack, praising him as the best person I know. He rolls his eyes.

"I don't know how you find the time to finish all these, Audrey. It makes me worry—you should be out and about in the city! You're still young!"

I bite my lip, suddenly wanting to tell Emil *everything*. He's been a part of my life for so long that it almost comes spilling out of me. Instead, I bite back the truth and tell a half-lie. "I'm—actually seeing someone right now. Kind of." Before he can get too excited, his eyes lighting up at the news, I add, "I'm not sure it'll work out."

"Really? Why not?"

"I don't know. He's just so..."

How do I explain Konstantin Martynov without giving

away who he is? He's infamous in New York; if I utter his name, Emil will know exactly how much danger I'm in and would probably call the cops right now.

"He's secure. A little older," I explain nervously, thinking of Konstantin's glittering silver hair and sharp eyes. A coil of anxiety and excitement settles in my belly.

"That's not always a bad thing," Emil muses. "As long as he can take care of you."

The words are reassuring, probably because I know that no matter how crazy all this is, Konstantin *can* take care of me.

Especially if I'm the mother of his child.

I reach out to take Emil's hand again, promising to stop by sooner and stay in touch. Then I heft the pile of books and start off toward work.

* * *

"Honestly, I thought they'd just offed you and were telling everyone you were sick to cover their tracks."

I roll my eyes at Chrissy, trying to focus on reconciling the last week's income through the shell companies. If you'd told me, during my years in college, that one day I'd be a money laundering aficionado, I would've thought you were crazy. But here I am.

"I really *was* just sick, Chris. It's not that serious."

"Still. Things were definitely weird around here," she drops her voice to a murmur, glancing over in the direction of the other pair of cubicles. "Duscha has been walking around like she's queen of the city. It's good to see that smile wiped off her face today, when you walked in."

I try to hide my own smile, dipping my chin down.

Duscha's expression when I stepped off the elevator was one of disbelief. She's the one who picked up on my "errors" and told Konstantin; he made that clear. So, she must be wondering what the hell I'm doing back at work and not floating in several different pieces down the Hudson.

A shadow looms over our desks.

My breath catches. Chrissy's chair rolls away.

Standing between us is...

Lev.

He's completely silent, staring down at me with a blank expression. Most people—especially Jeanette—find it disconcerting, how he never talks. But I swear there's something *more* to him. He can't just be a mindless soldier, or Konstantin wouldn't have picked him to lead the soldiers.

He holds out a folded over piece of paper.

I take it.

Then he disappears, boots silent on the tiled floor.

"What the hell," Chrissy whispers. I shoot her a warning look; better not to draw attention to how *completely weird* that interaction just was.

Slipping my finger between the paper, I unfold it and read, in flawless script: **There will be a car waiting out front at 5 p.m. Get in it.**

The car is a red Alfa Romeo, and it is definitely *not* inconspicuous. A handful of people are leaving or heading into the Spire, and they stare at me as I slip into the backseat nervously.

Chrissy texts me: **That's one of Mr. Martynov's cars, Audrey. What's going on?**

I should answer her, but I don't. Because what will I say?

Oh, I just agreed to let him fuck me until I'm knocked up because I was stealing thousands of dollars from him to pay off a debt I owe.

She would never look at me the same way again.

But clearly, Konstantin isn't worried about keeping this quiet.

I realize quickly that we aren't going to the cute little country home where I now live. Instead, the driver delves deeper into the city, until we reach a stunning townhouse on a tree-lined street.

It doesn't *look* like the leader of the Russian mob would live here, but I suppose that's the whole point.

The townhouse is painted a dark, almost midnight blue, with wrought iron fencing and window bars. Plants spill from the windowsills and create a kind of walkway to the front door, like stepping into a forest, the large pots ornate and heavy.

I reach the door, turn to look—the car is already gone.

People are walking the street slowly and casually. They obviously live here; there's no traffic at all, and the passersby are dressed so flawlessly that it feels like I stepped into a Vogue photoshoot.

The knocker is heavy, honey-colored wood, smooth under my already sweating palm. I knock and wait, feeling more nervous, possibly, than the day Konstantin told me in his office that he knew exactly what I had done.

The door opens and there's a... butler?

Does Konstantin Martynov have a butler?

The man is impeccably dressed. And expecting me, apparently.

"Miss Wolfe." He bows a little half-bow, and I feel suddenly out of place.

"Oh, you don't need to do that, Mr...?"

"You can call me Stanely, miss. Mr. Martynov is expecting you. This way, please."

Stanley leads me into a beautifully paneled, dark wood hallway, and then asks me to wait. He disappears *somewhere* into the massive townhouse, which must be at least four stories high.

Turning in a slow circle, I take it all in.

It's gorgeous. Dark. Woody. Smokey. It smells like a *man,* in a musky, spiced way that makes my blood pressure spike, but before I can peer into the next room he says my name from the top of the stairs.

"Audrey."

The sight of him, waiting for me, leaves me breathless.

Konstantin stands with his legs spread, hands in his pockets. The dark trousers he wears pull tight against his hips and his tie is undone.

I haven't seen him all day.

"Come."

Oh, I almost do, right there, at those words.

Taking a steadying breath, I try to walk up to him gracefully. It takes everything in me not to crawl the last few steps and beg him to *use me.* I hate how badly I want him, especially knowing that he got all this—this beautiful home, these opulent surroundings—by killing. Stealing.

Threatening.

Instead, I reach him, and he takes my hand, leading me down a hallway to an almost ridiculously large bedroom. It's the complete opposite of the bedroom in *my* home, or the home he made for me. Dark, brooding, elegant, but with little personality. I can't seem to look away from the bed.

Konstantin strips his tie off.

"Take off your clothes."

I practically jump to obey, toeing off my heels and lifting the simple pleated dress over my head. I *could* unbutton it, but there are at least fifteen buttons, and I can't help how badly I want—

What?

I want him to touch me. I want him to tell me what to do.

And as much as I hate admitting it, I want him to use me, to bury himself deep inside me until my pussy can't hold anymore of his cum.

"Leave the tights."

Before I can snap off the stockings from the garter belt, Konstantin's words make me freeze. He walks around me slowly, fingers ghosting up my back to undo the clasp of my bra effortlessly. It slides down my shoulders, to the floor.

He steps close, running his hands over the textured cut of the garter belt, down the straps to massage my thighs.

"These stockings... they drive me crazy at work. I was thinking about them all day."

"You were? I didn't see you... I thought maybe you weren't there..."

"I was watching, Audrey. I've been watching you for a long time."

The heat of his body is *so close* I can't help pressing my

ass back toward him, feeling the stiff trousers ghost against my skin before he hooks an arm around my hips and pulls me back.

"You didn't think you were done with work today, did you, my love?"

The endearment is almost too much, too early, and my chest feels tight. But my pussy throbs at the feel of his cock hardening against my ass.

Konstantin slips his fingers beneath my panties, delicately playing with my clit.

"You're already so wet."

I swallow, tipping my head back onto his shoulder as one hand plays with my pussy, the other palming my breast. I don't want to tell him the truth: that all day I've been anticipating when this will happen next.

When he'll demand more of me.

Abruptly, almost violently, he pulls my panties down my legs, leaving me in just the garter belt and stockings. The air in the room ghosts over my clit and my knees tremble for a moment.

"Bed."

I obey immediately, moving toward the bed, looking back over my shoulder when I'm unsure of how he wants me. He stalks toward me, pausing only to shuck off his clothing. He's not wearing boxers this time, and his cock springs free, thick, and bouncing against his thighs.

The memory of how it filled me up, how tight I felt around him, makes my pussy throb.

"Bend over. I want to take my time with you, Audrey, but I have another obligation tonight. So, you'll take me—all of me—and then I want you to lie here while my cum drips out of you. Do you understand?"

"Yes," I gasp, bracing myself against the bed as he turns me to face it.

Konstantin rams into me.

It should be painful, but I'm so wet and ready for him that it only makes me moan in satisfaction.

"You've been waiting for this, haven't you?"

He pounds into me, one hand gripping my hip, the other pulling my leg up onto the bed and opening me up. He changes the angle, and I gasp out again, "*Yes.*"

It's the only thing I can say as he growls commands and dirty questions.

"You like when I fuck you like this?"

Yes.

"You feel how badly I want you? How hard you make me?"

Yes.

"Are you ready for me, Audrey? I need you to take it like a good girl. Yes, just like that."

Yes, yes, yes.

He's so rough that pleasure and pain blend together until I'm practically screaming under him, my hips ramming back into his. His cock stretches me, the wet sound of every thrust bringing me closer to the edge.

"Just like that," he bites out, pushing me down between the shoulder blades and pinning me to the bed.

He grunts with each thrust, and as I recognize the quickening pace that means he's going to come, I find my own orgasm.

At the thought of him spilling into me. At the thought of

being bred by him, fucked until I'm pregnant, and then probably fucked more judging by just how voracious he is.

As he comes he moans in Russian, words I don't recognize and can't even grasp with my hazy mind. My body jerks forward with each slow thrust, reveling in the feel of his hand holding my ass down as he fucks into me.

Eventually Konstantin pulls out. I can't help the whimper I let out, wanting to feel his weight on top of me, his huge cock softening inside me.

"What did I tell you," he says gruffly. "Get on the bed."

Somehow, I manage to drag myself onto the king-sized bed and turn over, knees bent as I stare at the ceiling. Konstantin moves around outside of my field of vision, then comes back with a pillow. He uses it to prop up my hips.

Our eyes meet.

A dribble of cum spreads down from my pussy. He grins a slow, devilish grin, silver hair glinting in the city lights outside. Using his fingers, he gathers the cum and stuffs it back into my pussy roughly. My body tries to clench, useless with the aftershocks of the orgasm.

"Good girl. I want you to stay like that until I tell you that you can go."

I nod, sighing contentedly. Konstantin comes back with a warm rag and lays it between my legs but doesn't clean me up.

Not yet.

I can hear him dressing, and still mindless with satisfaction, I blurt out, "I'm surprised you sent a car for me right in front of the Spire. Everyone noticed."

His laugh is low, dark.

"You think I don't want them to know?"

His words make me freeze.

"You... you're okay with everyone finding out? That I'm yours?"

I prop myself up on my elbows, trying to find him in the dim light. His large shoulders and torso are backlit by the streetlamps. "You want them to know that we're... doing this?"

I don't say, *That you send a car for me after work to fuck me senseless.* I don't say, *That you're breeding me to carry your child, and I like it so much I'm wet all day at my chair, waiting for you to come get me.*

He turns, eyes serious and cold.

"They would find out one way or another, Audrey. And if they know, you can't run, can you? Because either they'd catch you, or I would. Which, do you imagine, is worse?"

The look in his eyes... it's what I imagine many men have seen in their last moments. He's like a predator, devoid of any emotion, and I feel like a piece of meat laid out on his bed.

"Olena Belov showed up at the house."

Turning away from me, he says only, "I know."

Tears gather at the corner of my eyes. I dash them away quickly, not wanting to see how this upsets me; that he doesn't care that his own associates are violating any privacy I might have, showing up to question me about what Konstantin wants with me.

What am I supposed to say to them?

It feels ridiculous to say that he wants just that: *me.*

That for some reason, he thinks I'm good enough to bear his heir.

"I'm sorry."

The shock his words bring stop the tears from coming.

"I told her she overstepped, and she understands. That is her way of looking out for me." He turns to face me, now dressed again, though in a different suit. It's beige, understated, and looks wonderful on him. Through the dress shirt it's easy to see how good of shape he's in, his chest like a rock, his tapered waist.

"She doesn't trust you."

I swallow, swinging my legs beneath me without thinking. "I understand."

Konstantin's eyes flicker to my now kneeing posture on the bed, and my heart thuds with fear.

I didn't wait for him to tell me I could move.

But his gaze slides away, and he gently gathers my dress and heels, setting them on the bed. "My driver is outside. You have two choices: he will bring you home. Or you can wait until I return from dinner. You can shower, get back in bed, and wait for me to come back."

He takes my chin in his hand, searching my face.

"I'll have more time to make this... worth your while."

His lips curl with the promise, beard ghosting my jaw as he lays a kiss just below my ear.

Konstantin Martynov disappears from the room, leaving me in the dark.

I should go home. Clean up. Curl up with my books.

But I know that I'll stay. He's like a drug and I'll let him destroy me, if only for the moments he makes me feel sublime.

Chapter 12

Konstantin

Olena sits on the edge of my desk, both of us watching the small screen that reflects the accountants' room.

Only minutes ago, we were discussing the operations branch of the business. Specifically, increasing the size of weapons shipments coming into Atlanta now that we've bought off law enforcement there.

Olena is sharp, though, and caught the way I kept glancing at my door. Flexing my hand. Rubbing my thigh.

"You're like a horny teenager," she chastises, annoyed. "Can't you think of anything else?"

"It'll be over," I promise her, "when there's a child. Then we can move on."

It's a promise I'm not sure I can keep, though, as I stare at Audrey on the screen. Specifically, at the way her shapely calves are crossed.

I've taken her almost every single night for the past week. First, in my townhouse. But I've since made the trip to the country house every night, almost cancelling plans on Tuesday to see her. Instead, I showed up close to one in the morning, woke her with my cock on her lips.

"You have to do it."

My gut twists with something like anxiety.

But I don't get anxious. Not over anything; declaring a man dead, killing him myself, torching a business that rebels.

Certainly not firing someone.

"She's good at what she does Olena."

"Right. Aside from stealing."

Her eyes go flat at my grin. "We are in the business of stealing. Perhaps she's only doing as she's taught."

Olena stands, the holster around her shoulders creaking as she does so. "You've made your point. Everyone knows she's yours. Your men have their orders; she hasn't been visited by anyone, right?"

"Aside from you?"

Her eyes flash now in anger, and I grunt back in annoyance, standing to pace the room. I despise how on edge I feel, how cornered.

I haven't felt like this since I was new to the city and fighting my way up the chain of command.

Earning my scars. Earning my place. Sending money back home, only to be met by silence.

"They haven't seen anyone following or watching her, no. What else have you found out about Sal Imperi?"

It wasn't hard to find out his name, not when the idiot made enough of a scene for a neighbor to file a police report.

"It appears he's known to them. For petty crimes in his youth, but larger issues recently. Only no charges have been pressed—he gets off every time. Same lawyer." She gives me a knowing look.

"Haymond?"

Olena nods.

Ron Haymond is a lawyer in deep with Giuseppe Sartorre's gang. He has a way of getting Giuseppe's best men off the hook. Which means Sal Imperi, despite his greasy appearance, is more important than he looks.

It can't be just a coincidence that he was dating Audrey just before she worked for me. But I can't step into Sartorre's territory and demand an answer; I need Audrey to give it up. To tell me just what kind of trouble she got herself into.

How else can I save her, if she won't tell me the truth?

"Fine," I agree, exhausted by the short argument and Olena's rock steady will. "Leave and send in Gorbichov."

Moments later, Allen Gorbichov enters. I give him a single order, with no explanation. He nods and executes it.

And then all hell breaks loose.

Hell is quite enticing.

Audrey stands in my office, fists clenched, breasts heaving beneath the flimsy polka dot blouse.

"How dare you."

She's already cursed me out, caused a scene. Even Lev turned his head once at her raised voice. My windows may frost as needed, but the room isn't soundproof; I've never needed it to be because *no one* disrespects me.

Until now.

"You can't fire me Konstantin and use me as your fuck toy. You can't have both!" She pushes a chair out of the way, stalking up to the desk, a wild look in her gorgeous eyes. I'm tempted to grab her throat and shut her up by covering those lush lips with my own.

"I'm not just going to take orders and let you destroy my life! I worked *hard* for this, I'm good at my job. You know it, or you wouldn't have hired me."

Standing abruptly, I momentarily silence her with the movement. Audrey takes an involuntary step back.

"Do you want to know why I hired you?"

I round the desk, slowly. Composed.

She's practically shaking with anger.

"I hired you because when I saw you at the construction site, I wanted to fuck your brains out. Right there, in the dirt."

All the color drains from her face.

I step toward her, yanking her to me by the blouse. Several buttons pop off and bounce across my desk.

"I hired you because the moment I saw you I wanted to wreck you. In front of all those men, if I could have the choice. I wanted to *own* your pussy."

My hand covers her shoulder, the junction where it meets her neck just above her collarbone. Applying pressure, I make it clear what I want from her.

If she resists I can crush the muscle.

Audrey stares into my eyes hopelessly, the anger extinguished by fear. She lowers herself until she's kneeling in front of me and I move my hand from her shoulder to her throat.

Banishing thoughts of what I could do to her from this angle, I focus on the task at hand: putting the fear of God—no, of Konstantin Martynov—in her.

"I own you, Audrey. If I decide you no longer work for me in this office, you no longer work for me. You are not to question this."

I drop to my haunches. Audrey flinches away from me, but I hold tight to her throat, putting just enough pressure that she can't pull away without hurting herself.

That's the lesson I want her to learn: *If she leaves, she's doing this to herself. If she leaves, I can't redeem her.*

"You've been lying to me. Since the day I brought you in here and made it clear that I knew you were stealing from me, you've lied."

"I—I didn't lie, I just can't tell you—"

"An omission is the same as a lie. *You* have been helping my enemies, Audrey. That's all I can assume if you refuse to tell me why you've stolen just shy of one hundred thousand dollars." I lean in close, tightening my grip enough that she stumbles forward on her knees to relieve the pressure. "I don't think it was a coincidence that you were at the construction site. Someone got lucky; they didn't know that I would decide you were mine. But they put you there for a reason, didn't they?"

Her eyes are glassy with fear, but her lips stay pursed, colorless.

Standing, I stare down at her, finally starting to get truly angry with her.

"Beg."

"Wh—what?"

103

She rocks back onto her heels, falls on her ass. It rucks up the pencil skirt she's wearing in an obscene way, her luscious thighs exposed.

"Beg me to give you mercy, and I might."

Swallowing, she whispers, "Please..."

I wait.

"Konstan—Mr. Martynov, please. Please forgive me. Or don't forgive me—" Audrey corrects quickly when she sees my hand flex, "—just give me some time to make things up to you. I can, I promise. I'll be good. I'll do what you say."

She drops her gaze to the floor.

The obedience from her shouldn't turn me on. It shouldn't satisfy me.

I would never, *ever* let anyone get away with what Audrey Wolfe has gotten away with.

"Stand up."

She does, almost falling, and I catch her by the elbow. Pulling her close, I breathe in the warm scent of vanilla and citrus. It stirs something like regret in me.

What is this woman doing to me?

It feels dangerous.

It feels good.

"Leave. You're done here."

Audrey sucks in a breath, stumbling away from me. She catches herself on the back of a chair and then walks quickly out of the room. I circle around the desk and watch the small screen. On it, she gathers her things quickly, not speaking when one of the accountants—Chrissandra Ives—begins to talk to her.

Lev watches from the hallway entrance.

Audrey practically runs to the elevator. I swear on the

feed I can see her shoulders shaking, though it isn't detailed enough for that.

Then she's gone.

* * *

It's just past midnight before I let the day's emotions flood in on me.

I've managed to keep them at bay through a meeting with my brigade leaders, each overseeing a territory of the city, and another with my informants.

I took a call from Dubai and spoke to the heads of my construction teams for project updates.

Yet still... my feelings for Audrey have been a wave barely kept at bay.

I stare at her name on my phone.

Malen'kiy volk.

My *little wolf.*

Something in me is breaking as I sink into an armchair overlooking the city. My entire life in America, I've taken satisfaction in wielding control over others. In making them beg, and cutting their lives short. Making them pay.

Today's episode with Audrey was satisfying... at first.

When I close my eyes, I see hers. The fear in them.

I want to destroy anyone who makes her feel that way. I want to be the kind of man to make her feel safe.

The phone rings twice before she picks it up, answering reluctantly. "Hello?"

She sounds sleepy, hushed. I imagine her in the bed: wrapped in the duvet, huddled up, scared.

"If you do what I say, I'll protect you. But you can't lie

to me anymore Audrey. If you carry my child, I'll never let anyone lay a hand on you. I'll burn this city down to do right by you. Do you understand?"

There's silence, but I know in the depth of the night that my words have sunk in.

I hang up.

Chapter 13

Audrey

It's the kind of fall day that has me restless. Laying on the couch in the country house, I flip over onto my side—again—and keep reading a weathered copy of *Wuthering Heights*. But reading about the misty, moody moors just makes me want to get out into the crisp sunlight.

With a sigh, I stand and drag myself into the kitchen, sweeping the beige linen dress around my ankles. Kashmere is in there prepping dinner. One of my favorites, unsurprisingly: lasagna. I take a deep breath, catching the comforting scent of yeast too.

"Are you making bread?"

She smiles at me over her shoulder. "Yes. Is that okay? To go with dinner?"

"That's *amazing*." Stretching across the island, I let my tired muscles tense and then relax, making a face at the knot in my back. Just *how* did I get so sore? From doing literally... nothing.

Kashmere shoots me a sideways glance. "Is there something I can get you, Miss Wolfe?"

"No, I'm fine, I'm just bored. Sorry, is it uncomfortable that I'm just in here watching?"

She shakes her head and gives me another small, kind smile. Eyes narrowed, I go back and forth in my head with a "should I/shouldn't I" as she tumbles the dough out of the bowl and begins to knead it. I haven't spoken to anyone from my personal life in a week, which I feel bad about—I shouldn't keep ignoring Chrissy's texts or giving her short answers. This is *embarrassing*, though, and definitely can't tell the few people I'm close to just what I've gotten myself into.

Except... if anyone might understand, it's Kashmere. From the dozens of questions, I pepper her with every day, I've found out that she's worked for Martynov Global for fifteen years and oversees every single service crew in the Tristate area.

So how the hell did she get stuck cleaning my sheets?

"Does it bother you to be here?" I ask out of the blue. Kashmere does a good job of looking like I didn't just give her whiplash with the awkward, intrusive question.

"Of course not, Miss Wolfe." She shapes the dough into a loaf and carefully tucks it into a bread pan.

"That's impressive," I murmur. "My grandma was a great baker. I never really took to it, I guess."

Her eyes are kind, and suddenly I feel the urge to cry, pushing it down.

"I only learned to bake because my husband loves muffins, and it was getting a little expensive."

A comfortable silence sets in, and after a bit I try again: "Shouldn't you be... I don't know. Coordinating all the employees that work under you, in an office somewhere? Overseeing scheduling, payroll, all that?"

This time, she doesn't look up. Her voice has a cool edge to it. "I have time enough to do that, before I come here. I rely on my management team. They're well trained." She looks up, and the look in her eyes makes me feel guilty for pushing her. "I enjoy what I do, Miss Wolfe. After all, I got into the service industry to serve."

"I'm sorry, Kashmere. I don't mean to be snippy, I just..." This is it; the make-or-break moment. If I tell her the truth about my situation, it could end badly—for me, for her. The loneliness I've felt for the past week settles in my chest, and I bite my lip. "I got let go from my job," I explain. "I worked for Mr. Martynov as an accountant. He fired me and now, he expects me to just stay here I guess."

I sit up, annoyance stoking the fire in me that hasn't felt so active lately. "I mean, what am I supposed to do, just wait for him to show up?"

Kashmere is watching me carefully. I can't quite tell, but have a feeling that she *might* know why I'm here... especially if she's cleaning the sheets.

The sheets that Konstantin has me fisting every time he shows up, commands me to spread my legs, and pounds into me.

Ugh. I shouldn't be turned on by the thought, especially with how frustrated I've been lately, but I am.

"Hmm. I understand; I'd have a hard time if I had to stop working, too." Her head tips to the side. "Can you go out at all? It's a beautiful day."

"It *is*." The afternoon sun is streaming in through the windows, leaves chattering in golden and red hues outside.

"I don't know though... I got a message earlier that he's coming here, so I need to be... available."

A blush heats up my cheeks, and Kashmere gives me a knowing glance.

Yeah, okay. She definitely knows what happens when our boss shows up at night, after she goes home.

"It would be a shame if he were to arrive and you weren't here." Her tone is neutral. I nod along, distracted by memories of fall growing up—picking apples with my grandmother. Hot cider, hot chocolate, the brisk air. "Well, I need to check in on one of the nearby properties. You'll be okay alone?" she asks, eyes twinkling. "I'll probably just walk, and leave my car here."

I stare, lips parted, as she gathers her things and leaves the bread for a final rise. Kashmere meets my eyes, puts her car keys on the kitchen island, and slips out the back door.

Surely she can't mean...

In seconds, I'm up and clutching the keys. The city isn't a far drive, and I'd love to walk the streets. Maybe find some comfy sweaters in a thrift shop or just pop into a café for a hot chocolate and a scone.

Feeling more energetic than I have all week, I slip on my kitten heels, take one last guilty look around the empty house, and lock the door on my way out.

Chrissy meets me at Spiced, a favorite café of ours, and I finally confess at least *some* of what has been going on. Or at least, I put a spin on it.

"You're *dating* our *boss!?*" she practically shouts, chai latte spilling from the to-go cup.

"Shhh!" There's no way any of Konstantin's associates are *here* of all places, in a café the size of a shoebox, but still.

"I mean, I saw the photo of you two out for dinner..."

"And what?" I ask sarcastically, rolling my eyes. "You thought it was a business dinner?"

She covers her mouth, staring into the distance. "I can't believe this Audrey. I can't believe you didn't tell me!"

I wince. "I know, I'm sorry. It just didn't seem like a good idea while I was still there." The words come out sour, bitter.

"Um, yeah. About that. You didn't seem too happy about being let go, so I'm assuming that wasn't a mutual choice?" She raises her brows.

"Yeah... not exactly. I mean, I get it." And I kind of do, now that I'm not trapped in the house. "If people knew we were seeing one another—"

--that he's fucking me into a mattress every night—

"—it would probably be a big issue with investors, his managers, you know. Everyone who sees Konstantin as... cold, calculated."

"A killer," Chrissy deadpans.

"Yeah. That too."

Leaning over the tiny table, she practically hisses, "Audrey, you're *sleeping with a murderer.*"

Not only that, I'm going to have his baby. My face heats up for the second time today at the thought of the things Konstantin does to me when we're alone.

And how much I like it.

God, I *like it.*

Checking one of the two phones on the table, I take a sip of my drink to avoid responding to that. Chrissy catches the action; I've already explained the whole "having two phones" scenario.

"So, is he going to be mad that you're out? If you guys had a date planned?"

Yeah, another little white lie; instead of telling her that he's coming over to the luxurious, curated home he put me up in to debauch me and knock me up, I told Chrissy that Konstantin and I *have a date.*

As if he's a totally normal guy, and not a Russian mafia leader.

"Mmm... he probably won't be thrilled," I admit, "but he'll get over it."

She shakes her head incredulously. The truth is, I know Konstantin will probably punish me for sneaking out. Am I mad about that? More annoyed than anything. Will I like it?

... yes.

Definitely.

"Come on," I say, standing. "I want to go to The Dog Ear, I'm dying to get a new book."

* * *

Half an hour later, Chrissy finally seems over the news. At least, she isn't staring at me with disbelief whenever I glance over the bookshelves. My arms are already full of books; five to be exact, and I know I'll have to slow down. But I also have Kashmere's car, parked two streets over, so I *could* splurge since I don't have to carry these home...

"There you are."

The voice is cold and familiar. A shiver goes up my spine, and I turn, pressing myself into the corner of the poetry section.

Sal is looking at me with a Cheshire cat smirk. I haven't seen him in weeks—not since the cops were called on him—and he looks worse for wear. His hair is shaggy, he has a five-o-clock-shadow, and a wild, stressed look in his eyes.

"Sal—"

Before I can say anything else, two men linger near the end of the bookcases on either side of this section. We're tucked far away from the register, in an area most people don't frequent.

No one notices Sal and his men crowding me in.

"Did you think I wouldn't come for you?" He steps closer, his breath sour and warm on my neck. "I told you, your debt is doubled. I don't care if you're his."

He moves closer, his thighs pressed against my pelvis, belt buckle digging into my stomach. *"You were mine first."*

Where the hell is Chrissy?

No—I don't want her to see this, to say anything to Sal and get tied up in this. Where's the manager? An employee? Anyone?

The books thump to the ground as Sal grips my wrist tight, jerking me away from the wall.

"What are you doing?" I gasp, dragged along as he maneuvers further back in the store. His men follow, silent and as dark as shadows as they move through the shelves. In moments we're at the back door and I stumble out into the alley.

"Sal—I didn't come alone, I—"

"Your friend can't help you," he scoffs, turning to face

me. His hair falls into his eyes, still wild with anger and excitement. "That money, Audrey. A stupid bitch like you won't be able to scrape up that much, so I'm going to try another way. Do you really think he believes you're *worth something*," he taunts, mimicking the words I said the night we fought in my apartment.

"Would he pay for you, Audrey? Buy you back like a piece of property?"

He jerks me closer to him, the movement making me cry out at the pain in my wrist.

"You slut," he hisses. "You think I don't know what you've been doing with him? You'll get on your knees for anyone, won't you?"

My heart is pounding so hard I think I might pass out.

Before Sal can say anything else, a fist comes out of nowhere and catches him in the jaw so hard he falls against the brick building.

"*Fuck!*"

The sounds of a fight draw my attention, and suddenly Lev is there, taking out Sal's two goons easily with a baton.

But it's not just Lev.

Konstantin steps into view, his face impassive as he stares at Sal, half-crumpled against the wall. The brick has scraped away a patch of skin on his face and he's already bleeding.

Wordlessly, Konstantin reaches out and grabs Sal by the hair. Sal screams, stumbling into the Bratva leader.

Seeing the two of them so close is shocking. Konstantin makes Sal look like a sack of meat, inelegant and coarse as he curses. Konstantin lands another punch, effortlessly, and a crunch sounds out.

Sal falls back, dazed. His nose is badly crooked, blood pouring down it and soaking into his shirt. Nausea makes my mouth water. I turn away, turn into Konstantin's outstretched arm.

"Malen'kiy volk."

"A fuggin' ped name," Sal slurs through the blood. "She has you whipped Martynov. She's not worth it." He's swaying on his feet but still facing Konstantin—braver than I expected.

The crunch of gravel signifies Lev's arrival; he stands just behind and to the side of us, eyes on Sal. When I glance back, I see two bodies on the ground and blood soaking into the asphalt and stone.

Sal straightens, chin raised.

Oh, God. He's squaring up as if ready to meet his maker. It's both ridiculous and gut-wrenching, and before I can stop myself I ask: "Let him go, please. He's not worth it."

Konstantin's body is rigid against me as I tuck myself close to his side. He doesn't look at me or acknowledge what I've said, but a slow smile breaks across his face.

"Go running back to your owner, dog," Konstantin says coldly.

Sal's eyes narrow. He looks from Konstantin to me, and then to Lev. Then he laughs.

"Damn. She really has you pussy whipped, old man."

Konstantin's hand flexes, and for a moment I think he'll change his mind. But Sal stumbles off down the alley, breaking into a run, and disappears around the corner.

A large arm wraps me closer.

I bury my face in Konstantin's wool jacket, pretending that the itchy fabric is what's making my eyes water.

"Can we go home?" I whisper.

He gently grips my chin and makes me look at him. His eyes are serious, brows furrowed. "Will you stay there? If I take you home?"

Knowing that I'm willingly sealing my fate, to be *his* and only his, I nod.

The wool coat lays across an armchair, waiting for Kashmere to take care of it—tomorrow.

Konstantin sent her home with a short text when we returned to the house, Lev parking her car in the drive and then disappearing into the tree line nearby.

"It was my idea," I insist, following Konstantin upstairs. "She didn't have anything to do with it."

"Saving everyone today, aren't you?" he grunts out, eyes flashing as he strips off his tie and shirt. The sight of his bare chest, sprinkled with dark hair and ridged with muscle, makes my gut clench. "I should have killed that boy," he scoffs. "Should have let Sartorre find his body with the others."

Guilt floods through me.

He's right; things with Sal could've ended right there. I bite my lip, keeping the secret, because they wouldn't *really* have ended. I still owe money, and *someone* would come for it, whether Sal was breathing or not.

Konstantin takes my hips, maneuvering me into the master bath. I don't say anything as he strips off my dress, letting it pool to the floor. There are flecks of Sal's blood on his throat and I stare at it as he bares me to the already-warming air, the shower running.

"Get in."

I obey. I don't think I could disobey now if I wanted to.

In the shower, I let the water run over my face, then move forward and let it soak into my hair. Eyes closed, I feel Konstantin step in behind me. His bare body brushes against my skin, making it goosepimple even in the warm water. He slips an arm around my waist.

"Will you listen now, and stay here?" Dipping his head lower, he runs his lips up my neck. "I can't protect you if you're always running, Audrey."

I make a sound of agreement, but then open my eyes, remembering this morning's frustration. "I'm... bored here, Konstantin." Turning, I try to focus on keeping eye contact.

And not looking at the very obvious distraction now pressing insistently against my thigh...

"Mmm, I'm not keeping you occupied enough, am I?"

His hand delves down, between my thighs, seeking out the beginnings of how badly I want him. I widen my stance, bracing my hands against his shoulders and giving him access.

"No," I continue, somewhat mindlessly as his thumb ghosts over my clit. "I'm serious, I need something to take up my time now that I'm not working." Shooing his hand away in annoyance, I add, "If you want.. *that,* let's just do it, please. Today was a lot."

I try to pull him closer with a hand on the back of his neck. While shower sex is definitely not my thing, a man like Konstantin—massive, muscled, and steady as a rock—

gives me a newfound confidence in climbing onto his hips. Before I can boost myself up, he holds me firmly by the hips.

"No, no, *malen'kiy volk*. There's no rushing this."

Whining half in protest and half from the way my pussy clenches when he squeezes my ass, I try to wriggle away. But Konstantin's grip only tightens, and he gets on his knees, the spray from the water glistening in his silver hair.

I want to protest, but he presses his mouth to my clit, kisses it so gently that my hips chase after him as he pulls away.

"Haven't you heard," he murmurs, that slow smirk shooting a thrill to my core, "that women who orgasm are more likely to conceive?"

The statement surprises me enough that I blurt out, "I'm not sure that's true."

Konstantin chuckles, hooking my knee over his shoulder and pulling me closer roughly. "We'll have to find out." One slow, long lick drags a moan out of me. "I'm planning on making you come over, and over, and over. As many times as it takes, Audrey."

One hand against the wall and the other in his hair, I just can't find it in me to put up a fight.

Chapter 14

Konstantin

The warehouse is an hour and twenty minutes outside of the city. The area is beautiful if you like wild things; the river with its white froth, trees as wide as four men, acres of field and far-off houses.

It reminds me too much of Russia, but without the desolation this season brings there. My stomach knots at the memory of being hungry. Of my mother shouting at one of her boyfriends when the heat was turned off. Of my brother crying.

The city pulls me back, as well as the *malen'kiy volk.* Tucked away in her house, safe, satiated hopefully. She's had to wait another week for me to make a decision.

Whether or not I like the country doesn't matter. It's the perfect place for a warehouse, and the large building looms as the SUV turns down a dirt drive. In one week, it will be paved. In three, we'll be moving high-end art through here for auctions. And housing black market items here as well, in the depths of the hidden rooms that only two men other than me know about.

The driver opens the door of the SUV, and I step out, Lev close behind, coming around from the passenger side. He stands just behind me, silent, watching. Interestingly, the country doesn't seem to make him nervous the way it unsettles me.

"Right this way, Mr. Martynov." A young man in a tailored but cheap suit gestures toward the main entrance, all steel and glass. I watch approvingly as he demonstrates impeccable manners. Inside, the manager of the warehouse, Antosha, greets us.

"Mr. Martynov. It's a pleasure to have you visit in the final stages."

Taking in the surroundings, I nod toward the young man, who disappears around a corner. "Is that the boy whose father died in an accident at the Dubai site?"

"Yes," Antosha confirms.

"And he's doing well?"

"He is. We've made sure he and his mother are well taken care of. He's bright; sharp. He realizes that the physical labor his father took part in is not the way he wants to go."

A sadness settles over me. Despite the violence of my occupation, it's hard when any of our men die, in accidents or otherwise. "Make sure he's taken to purchase a new suit. Or rather, four; and shoes. At my expense."

Antosha half-bows. "Of course, Mr. Martynov. Come, we can go to my office."

At the very back of the building it's possible to hear—and see, through three large glass windows—the airstrip that will bring the illegal goods in. A clear-cut path through the woods is being prepared by workers, creating easy transport right to the warehouse.

"To what do I owe this visit?" Antosha asks, sitting only after I'm seated. Lev remains by the door, his eyes taking in every inch of the new surroundings.

"I'm changing the plans. This location will have a direct accountant to answer to. She will be working off site, and will handle payroll, payment for goods and transportation, revenue."

Antosha nods, not questioning the oddity of having an accountant directly connected to this one warehouse. I could, if I wanted to, justify the choice: this will be one of the largest black-market houses on the east coast. We're expecting revenue in the first year to touch just under five billion. As an auction house, handling the cash will be complicated.

And it will give Audrey something to do, something to own. A way to feel utilized and engage her sharp mind.

However, none of my choices need justification.

"I'm assuming someone will reach out to set up the particulars?"

"Yes. Miss Belov will be in touch."

A flash of surprise crosses his face at the mention of Olena. Until now, I've let other managers handle the setup of this operation; handing it off to Olena means that it's truly important. And that the *accountant* is the important thing will not go unnoticed by Antosha. He's smart and won't say anything; won't ask any questions.

He only nods.

We spend a few minutes on updates, going over the main purchases I want to focus on in the first three months, naming some families overseas who might be interested in what we can bring in from Canada's west coast. Less than half an hour after arrival, Lev and I walk back toward the SUV.

In the car I put the privacy glass up. This phone call is not one I'm looking forward to, and it's unusual for her to be the last to know of these changes.

I tap Olena's name, and it rings only twice before she picks up silently.

"Olena. There's been a change of plans to the Hudson Valley Auction House." Filling her in on the details, keeping it short, I can sense the growing tension over the line.

"And who is this accountant?" she asks.

When I don't answer, she continues: "So then, this is a play to keep your pet entertained."

"Watch yourself, Olena," I snarl. Nerves make me quick to anger. It's been over a month since I made Audrey mine.

Maybe it's too late.

Maybe I *can't* have an heir. Forty-eight looks good on me, but that doesn't mean it hasn't affected certain... parts of me.

I end the call with Olena, but the anxiety still festers in me, making my skin itch. That voice from all those years ago keeps sounding in my head, whispering darkly: ***Why would you deserve it? Why should you have happiness? You are nothing, and you will have nothing to live for.***

My hand shakes as I make another call.

Audrey picks up, sounding sleepy. "Are you okay?"

I ask.

"'m fine," she murmurs, making something in me go soft at the airy sound of her voice. "Just tired. I took a nap."

"I'll be there in an hour," I tell her. "Be ready."

At the house, I gesture for the driver to remain in the car and open the back door myself. Audrey comes down the walkway, curious and wary all at once.

She looks gorgeous with her hair up in a tight bun, her thighs shown off in workout pants and a long sweater accentuating the color of her eyes.

Before she can duck into the car, I take her hand and turn her slowly, eyes dragging over her body.

"You're stunning," I murmur, satisfaction setting in at the rise of a blush on her chest.

"Thank you." She sways forward, then seems to catch herself, sliding into the SUV. "Where are we going?"

Was she going to kiss me?

My gaze drops to her lips.

Would I let her?

It's the one thing I've held back from. I'll do anything, everything else to her—but kiss her.

"You'll see."

The driver pulls away, heading for the city. Audrey watches the suburbs go by and I watch *her,* looking for any sign that my plan might have taken root.

But she looks... gorgeous, as ever. No different than the first day I saw her. What would there be to look for? From what I've read, Audrey would notice the very first signs, and she hasn't mentioned anything.

We pull up to a lavender and black Victorian on the outskirts of the city. It's been impeccably restored, and the windows reflect the fluttering leaves of the trees. A sign out front reads **The Vyatka Group,** and when Audrey turns to me quickly, I know she recognizes the name.

It was one of the accounts she used to oversee.

"This is where you'll work," I explain. "It's a short drive from the house, as you've seen. One of my men will pick you up every morning at 8 a.m. Your day will end at 3 p.m." My eyes sweep over her, still hoping for a sign. "I want you to rest, not to overwork yourself. Understand?"

Her brows furrow, lips pursed, and I almost wish she'd stolen that kiss earlier.

"Um, Konstantin... I'm not a realtor."

I point out the second floor of the building, explain that it's office space for my staff to rotate through as needed. "But you will have a dedicated office. Anything you need. If you'd like to start planning today, here is the number of the office manager. She'll get whatever you want."

Audrey lunges across the car, wrapping her arms around my shoulders. I sit stock still for a moment, then let my arm slide around her waist, breathing in her scent: that vanilla, citrus, spice that stirs something in me.

I find myself longing for her bed at the country house. I've started to think of it as *our* bed, the one place I truly lose myself. In her, in the possibility of a future.

A tap on the privacy glass starts the car moving again. As we drive through the city, Audrey listens, enrapt, as I explain her duties as the accountant for the auction house.

There's a brightness I haven't seen, a fire in her, since she confronted me at the Spire.

This is what I should've done all along: whatever it takes to make her happy. I find more satisfaction in her thorough questions and the way she squeezes my hand than the millions of dollars that roll into my accounts.

"Wait..."

The car stops and she realizes where we are. For a moment, something like fear flashes in her eyes. The Dog Ear's banner flutters in the autumn breeze, and Audrey doesn't move when the driver opens the door.

I get out, walk around to her side, and hold out a hand.

"You never finished shopping that day. I'd like to buy you whatever you want."

Tentatively, she takes my hand and steps out. When we're inside, she looks at me questioningly. "Where is everyone?"

The store is completely empty and impeccably kept. Even I find the shelves compelling and look over the signs quickly for the reference section. If she's distracted perhaps I can find something on conception, on best practices for those trying to conceive... my heart races at the idea of making a child with her, this woman whose hand is tucked into mine so easily as she gazes around us.

"The owners have been compensated for an hour's time. I hope that's long enough. Whatever you take will be paid for." At my gesture, she grins and moves among the shelves, eyes scanning.

"My Nana would've loved this," she laughs quietly, slipping out a book and cradling it in her arms. "She's the one who got me started reading. Well, *she* read to me from her books—all old classics mostly. That's the only thing, I could never talk her into trying anything new." She shakes her head, laughing again, and the sound breaks something inside me. I only realize I'm staring when Audrey shyly drops her gaze.

"Sorry, I... I have a hard time not talking or thinking about her, and this just..." She shrugs.

"Don't apologize," I murmur, voice rough with grief of my own; thoughts of Mikhail and the things he loved are never far away. "Even losing someone, they never really leave. You can find them..." I tip my chin toward the rest of the store, quiet and waiting for her, "...in places like this. Even when you aren't looking."

Her eyes glisten for a moment, then she looks away. I worry that I might've said the wrong thing, but before I can leave her, Audrey slips her hand into mine again.

"Will you stay?" she asks quietly, so close that I can feel her words against my lips. "Tonight, will you stay with me?"

Drawing a knuckle gently down her jaw, I lean in enough to ghost my mouth over hers. When she sways forward, I let myself give in: capture her in a kiss, sink into the bliss of peace and stillness.

"If that's what you want," I murmur, ignoring the sensation that I can't catch my breath.

I know that whatever she asks, I'll do.

Whatever she wants, I'll give her.

Chapter 15

Audrey

Even with my eyes closed I know the windows are open. The birdsong is louder, clearer, and I can smell fall: earthy, smokey, hinting at the rich loam under layers of leaves and the neighbor's woodstove.

There's a warmth closer that I gravitate toward.

Turning over, I burrow further into the bed.

Konstantin is like an ember. He gives off heat that draws me like a moth, and I can't help opening my eyes and slipping an arm over his waist. There's something in me that obsesses over the dips of each muscle, the trail of hair that leads down, beneath the sheet. His cock twitches with interest and I stifle a laugh.

It's crazy to think that once I feared this man. I mean, *genuinely* feared him.

Every single time I stole money out of his accounts, found a way to hide the transfers, the sense that I was a prey animal never left me. I was always waiting for him to notice.

Waiting for him to find me.

Sure, that he would destroy me.

Konstantin takes a deep breath and stretches, muscles tensing deliciously under my curious fingers. I find what I'm looking for and wrap my hand firmly around his shaft, feeling it harden to steel beneath my touch. There's something so powerful about having him like this, about the way he fucks me and owns me.

His eyes barely open. But his arm shoots out, wraps under my waist, and pulls me on top of him. Right away I can feel his hardening cock nestled between my thighs, and it makes me wet with anticipation. As Konstantin grumbles a "Good morning," I feel it more than hear it from the depths of his chest.

That's when I realize...

What I'm feeling isn't just lust. It's not just hazy, dopamine-induced attraction.

I don't just *want* Konstantin Martynov physically.

Somewhere deep down inside, a part of me longs for this. Waking up next to him. Being wanted, touched, and cherished. Wanting it to be *more* than just physical.

This is just another job, a small voice whispers in my head as Konstantin cards his fingers through my hair. ***All you are is a surrogate; somewhere for him to plant his seed.***

And when he gets what he wants, you're gone. You asked for it yourself.

I stop breathing, wishing the feeling away—the feeling of affection that's burying itself deep inside me.

"Um, I'm going to get up," I mumble, sliding carefully off of him and standing up.

He stares up at me, his dark brown eyes flashing caramel in the morning light.

"Audrey—"

"I just need to go to the bathroom. And I'm starting work today, I shouldn't be late," I say lamely, disappearing into the bathroom.

I *am* starting work today, but there's no need to rush— it's 6:45 a.m., and I'm pretty sure Kashmere made lunch for me. I already know there are scones, cream, and fruit downstairs. She doesn't usually come in before noon when Konstantin stays here; I'm not sure how she knows. He must text her, or have someone reach out to her, since last night was definitely unplanned.

I stare at myself in the mirror, tousled and sleepy. My chest aches realizing that I look happy, calm, dare I say fertile? Ugh. Healthier might be more accurate; definitely healthier than I looked when I was putting up with Sal and stealing from my boss instead of sleeping with him.

With a sigh, I run the water to drown out my thoughts. Somewhere in the bedroom Konstantin is making noise, and all I can do is pray that he doesn't come in here and make me feel all loved up. I don't think I could take it.

Fifteen minutes later, the bedroom is empty.

"Oh," I whisper, the air going out of me.

I should be happy he left. So why do I feel so bereft?

Dressing quickly, I wiggle into a wool pencil skirt and a simple ochre blouse. No heels today since I'm not sure if there's an elevator in the old Victorian, and don't want to chance narrow stairs. Nana used to work for a company in a

Victorian house, and she always complained about her knees at the end of the day.

Another pang in my chest. When did I start feeling so lonely? Or rather, when did it start bothering me like this?

Downstairs, the sound of silverware makes me freeze in the foyer. I turn the corner slowly and head toward the kitchen.

Maybe Kashmere *did* come in? Maybe Konstantin was planning on leaving all along and told her to get to work.

But instead, I find *him* in the kitchen, spooning cream onto a scone.

He looks up, eyes dark again and locking me in place. Something in me clenches at the look he gives me; the juxtaposition of such a hard man delicately swirling sweet cream over the baked good, a pile of strawberries in a bowl next to him.

God, I hate how much I want this.

"I don't have time to eat," I say, hearing the irritation in my voice and wincing internally.

Konstantin goes still. He watches me hurry to the fridge and dig around for the lunch Kashmere packed. A hummus sandwich, fresh grilled veggies making my stomach growl.

I hope he didn't hear that...

It's obvious when I turn around that he did. Konstantin's eyes narrow, and *this* must be how it feels to be on the receiving end of being hunted down by him—the leader of a crime syndicate.

"Did something upset you?"

His voice is frosty, forearms flexed as he leans against the counter.

"No," I answer shortly. "I just need to get going."

I glance out the window, but the car isn't here yet of course. Won't be for another forty minutes at least. There's definitely time to eat, time to play house, time for him to fuck me right here on the counter if he wants to.

My desire for him throbs at the thought and I push it down.

"Audrey." He catches me by the wrist, making me drop the pretty floral lunch bag. I huff and try to step away, but Konstantin pulls me close.

Not the way he did this morning, in bed.

He's glaring down at me. Angry.

I know why; I'm acting crazy. Irrational. Pushing him away when I practically begged him to come last night, figuratively and literally...

"We need to talk," he growls.

"I don't want to talk."

"Too bad." He jerks me closer. I let out a pained sound, but it doesn't hurt; not physically, at least. I don't want to talk. I don't want to get to know him better, or let him in.

I don't want to get attached and then leave... just like I requested.

A one-way ticket to the west coast.

A child left behind.

Is it freedom if all I ever think about is this place is him, and our potential child?

"I wanted to give you time to calm down," Konstantin says. "You were scared. When they came after you. But I need answers, Audrey. I need to know who Sal Imperi is to you, and why you were working with him."

"I wasn't working with him—"

It's not a lie, not exactly.

Konstantin doesn't like my tone. He calmly puts a hand on my throat, his thumb in the dip between my clavicles. It grounds me, but it shouldn't. I shouldn't like to be held like this, steadied, made to obey.

"I wasn't working with him," I grind out, teeth clenched. My eyes search his; I know he isn't letting me walk away from this conversation.

He gave me this job, and he can take it away. Doesn't matter if I'll be late. He can just fire me all over again.

Make me disappear, if he wanted to.

Could he do that? To someone he's been buried inside? Someone he's commanded to come, over and over?

"I... I borrowed money," I whisper, watching his walls crack just a little. "I borrowed money from Sal. I had to. I met him while my grandmother was sick, and he took advantage..."

His eyes light with anger and I hurry on, wanting to take the focus away in case he does something stupid, like go after Sal to finish him off this time. "When I started seeing him and he offered the money for her hospice care, I thought he was being nice. Caring. I didn't realize it was the mob's money, and I wasn't thinking, I couldn't let my Nana go into an institution. She wanted to stay home."

I trail off, the memories flooding in. I've worked so hard to keep them away for the past year, but now I feel it all over again: the grief of mourning someone before they're gone. Nana had always been so strong, opinionated; she would have hated Sal if she'd been in her right mind. But back then, when she looked at me, she looked *through* me. The pain took her away before she ever really passed.

"A few months after her funeral, Sal made it clear that I had to pay back the money. With interest."

When I don't say any more, afraid of what other secrets I might spill, Konstantin says: "So you started working for me."

"Yes."

I don't say that it was Sal's idea, that he got me the job at the construction site.

I don't say that he's the one who casually suggested I could skim money, little by little. That a man like Konstantin Martynov wouldn't miss a couple grand.

I don't say that the interest caught up quickly, and "little by little" wasn't enough.

"You didn't finish paying the debt," he says rather than asks.

I nod.

"Is that why he keeps coming for you?"

,I nod again, pursing my lips tight to keep the other half of the truth in, that for some reason, Sal wants Konstantin. It's clear now that getting to Konstantin has always been his goal.

But why? Surely Sal's boss can't be stupid enough to try to take out the leader of the Martynov empire?

Letting his hand drop from my throat to my chest, then to my waist, Konstantin slips two fingers into the waistline of my skirt. He tugs it, pulling me closer gently. His lips ghost my ear.

"Do you want to go back to him?" he whispers. "Do you miss him?"

I shake my head, throat thick with emotion.

That's the last thing I want.

Nipping my earlobe, Konstantin turns me until I'm backed up against the counter. I feel like a prey animal again, body trembling.

I like it.

"If I find out that you're with him, I'll gut him. I'll make you watch. And then I'll make it clear that you're mine, *malen'kiy volk*. Do you understand?"

"I... I don't want him," I stutter, pressing my thighs together to try to relieve the pressure of how badly I want him right now. How badly I want him to *claim* me.

"I just want you," I whisper.

Konstantin pulls back, frowning at my confession. I can't help myself and let the rest pour out: "I've wanted you since I started working at the Spire," I admit. "Even when I was with Sal, all I could think about was you."

He steps away, eyes scanning me as if looking for a lie.

He won't find one.

"You're not telling me everything," he finally grunts. I crouch down to pick up my lunch bag, not attempting to answer. He's right; I'm not telling him everything.

I can't tell him the truth—that I'm starting to fall for him.

The sound of a car arriving draws our attention. Konstantin slicks back his hair, fingers dancing down his buttons quickly.

For a moment, I imagine an alternate reality where he comes to me, kisses me. Promises to celebrate my first day when I get back by stripping off my clothes and making me come on his face.

But reality is harsh; he barely gives me a second glance

before striding toward the front door, opening it, and disappearing.

Chapter 16

Konstantin

The security system alerts me that someone has entered the front door, and I glance up from looking through the auction house's portfolio. There are a few items in it I might want for myself; one is a toy that my brother and I had when we were growing up. I'd found it for him, discarded on the street, and brought it home. Mikhail's smile swims in my memory as I stand and go to the wall, hitting a button that reveals a hidden screen.

There are two people in my foyer.

Lev doesn't surprise me, though he should be making the rounds at the nightclubs with his men and collecting dues.

But the sight of Audrey Wolfe in a silky nightdress does something to me that I can't explain.

A rush of hot anger, worry, and exasperation runs through me.

The woman can't listen. *Won't* listen.

Or she just likes the things I do to her when she disobeys. Miss Wolfe is quite responsive to spanking. The thought brings a short-lived smile before I head for the staircase, shoes echoing on the steel.

"Why did you bring her here?" I ask, staring at Lev and ignoring Audrey completely.

She opens her mouth to speak, but a quick look silences her. My gaze drops to her feet; she's wearing only house slippers embroidered with flowers, arms wrapped around herself against the chill night air.

I want nothing more than to take her in my arms. That realization sends another shot of worry through me.

Worry for her, but also worry because I'm getting too close.

Too comfortable.

It's been over a month and fucking her relentlessly should have taken the edge off my infatuation. Instead, I find myself thinking of excuses to go there—and now, avoiding it whenever I can.

Lev has been typing out a response on his phone, and he holds it out for me for me to read. That catches my interest. He could just play the audio, but for some reason this answer merits the respect of silence.

She needs to speak to you about her condition.

My eyes cut to her immediately, searching.

"Are you sick?" I ask, stepping toward her.

She shakes her head, biting her lip. "No, I..." Glances at Lev.

I send him away with a silent gesture. He opens the door and leaves. He'll be close by, or he'll get on with his evening. I'm not thrilled that he brought her here and she can tell.

"I reached out to him. You gave me his number for emergencies, and I... I needed to see you tonight."

Warmth blooms in my chest.

She *needed to see me.* I hate how much I like that, how much I want that. Her needing me.

"I'm pregnant," she whispers.

I have no words.

There *are* no words.

All my hopes, all my desperation, coalesces into this moment. Everything I've fought for, everyone I've had to stomp into the ground to make it here, every terrible thing I've had to do—it's worth it.

Abruptly, I reach for her and scoop her into my arms. Audrey lets out a yelp. The silk of her nightdress is buttery against my skin as I carry her upstairs, up to my bedroom, kicking the door shut behind us.

I lay her on the bed and carefully climb over her, pressing a hand carefully to her belly. It's warm, plush, as usual, but somewhere in there is the beginning of my legacy. And she has given this gift to me.

"You're sure?" I ask, awe in my voice.

Audrey's cheeks go pink as she nods. There's worry in her eyes.

"Are you okay?" I swallow before adding, "Do you... regret this?"

Slowly, silently, she shakes her head.

"No."

I can't hold back any longer. I wrap an arm around her waist and pull her close, kissing her deeply. She makes a contented sound against my mouth, her hands going to my neck.

Feeling a surge of what can only be affection and obsession, I cage her in and roll us, settling her on top of my hips. Audrey chuckles, but the way she grinds against my erection tells me she wants it just as badly as I do.

Is she as ecstatic as I am?

As in awe?

"Take it," I mumble, raising my hips to create more friction. "Take whatever you want, my little wolf."

She lets out a quiet whimper, reaching between us and lifting onto her knees to fumble at my sweatpants. I grin up at her torturously as she struggles. With a huff, Audrey backs down the bed and yanks until my cock springs free. She licks her lips greedily.

"No boxers?"

Foregoing an answer, I help her climb back on top, and this time when she grinds against me all I feel is wet heat.

I stare up at her in surprise.

"No panties?"

She laughs, then loses focus, pupils blown out as she teases herself with my cock. She throws her head back, gyrates until my shaft is slick with her need, and I'm gritting my teeth.

"If you keep doing that, woman, this is going to be over before it begins."

She smirks. It's a look I haven't seen yet, and I know I'll crave it from now on—that naughty glint in her eye as she reaches down, pumps me in her hand, thumb swiping over the head of my cock. I buck my hips at the sensitivity, cursing. "*Blyat'*."

With two hands on my chest, Audrey settles herself into place before taking me in one swift motion. She gasps and I clutch at her hips, the sensation of being enveloped in hot silk taking me over.

"Yes. Just like that," I encourage as she rides me shamelessly. "Good girl."

I wrap a hand into her hair, tugging until her nipples peak under her nightdress. The sounds are sloppy, indecent, and they only make me harder.

"You did such a good job. You like when I fill you up, little wolf? You like fucking me over and over?"

"Y-yes," she stutters out, changing the angle in a way that has me cursing again. "I want you to come inside me, Konstantin, please."

Propping myself up, I tense my abs as her clit grinds against my torso. She lets out small whimpers and gasps, no longer bouncing up and down but rotating her hips quickly, chasing her orgasm.

"Good girl. I'm going to make you come, Audrey, for doing exactly what I asked. For giving me what I want. Do you want that?"

"Yes!"

The sound of my hand slapping her ass is loud in the room. Her pussy gushes, squelching as she rides me.

"Good. Keep taking me, just like that. Fuck. I'm going to give you everything. Anything you want."

It takes everything in me not to flip her over, fuck into her relentlessly.

"You're mine," I grunt, tugging her close to me as she takes every inch of me. "Mine, Audrey. I'll give you everything. I'll destroy myself, for you."

The words stream out of me, mindless as I worship her, as her tits bounce and I bury my face in them. One bite is all it takes; light, my fingers pinching her nipple, and then she comes, crying out, hips stuttering. I can't stop myself from spilling into her, cock throbbing as her pussy tightens.

She's mine.

I meant every single word I said.

Even as I wish I could take them back.

Chapter 17

Audrey

"I insist."

I stare at Konstantin, not sure what to make of this. When I texted him earlier in the week to tell him that today was my first ultrasound appointment, I assumed he wouldn't come.

It's 10 a.m. on a Wednesday. Surely he has better things to do. I say that out loud, not meaning to, and his eyes darken.

"There is nothing more important than this."

The words are like an arrow, making my chest hurt. I hate how much I want him to mean it; how much I ache for him to be here with me. And he is.

We walk into the clinic and it's clear that they know exactly who he is. The receptionist drops her gaze immediately. I didn't tell them who the father was, but I didn't have to—Konstantin had his people make this appointment.

Aurum Wellness, when I looked it up, is *exclusive*. Almost impossible to get into. It caters to New York's elite and has quite a few clients who fly or drive in from across the country. The interior is flawless, all dark wood and dove-gray walls. There's an area for water, espresso, tea— served by a woman behind the counter.

We check in with the receptionist, who shoots a look at Konstantin but is obviously too scared to make eye contact. Konstantin is looking around as if inspecting his soldiers. He's critical, intimidating, and cold.

They don't ask for his identification. Instead, the receptionist whispers to me, "If you want to, you can just skip the part about the father. Unless... there are any genetic, um, issues you feel should be included."

Her voice gets higher, more nervous, when she realizes that Konstantin has heard her. He stares her down. But she has a point, and when we sit to fill out the paperwork, I murmur: "*Is* there anything I should know about? Any chronic conditions...?" When he's silent, I prompt as a peace offering, "My mom's side of the family is prone to diabetes. I dodged that bullet. Also... we have weak ankles," I joke, stifling a smile when he only raises a brow.

Gently, he takes the clipboard from me and purses the section on the background of the father. He makes a few short notes; nothing crazy, but I scan the information and see that he's checked off asthma, high cholesterol, and no drug or alcohol use.

"You had asthma?" I ask, the question popping out of me in surprise.

"My brother," he says gruffly.

"I... didn't know you had a brother." There's a pull in me to ask more. To find out where his family is—if he's still in contact with them. If he misses them. I haven't heard anything about Konstantin Martynov's family; not even rumors, which is suspect.

But now isn't the time. The door opens and a nurse calls us in, brings us into a small but comfortable room, and lets me know how I should undress and arrange myself.

It's... awkward, to say the least. Konstantin doesn't avert his eyes as I slip my underwear off under the button-down dress I'm wearing and slide onto the exam table, covering myself in the drape before pulling the skirt up.

He reaches out, a warm hand on my knee under the drape.

"You're comfortable?"

I nod, taking in my surroundings. I get regular annual visits, but I've never had an ultrasound before. The machine looks surprisingly small, but complex, with a little roller ball in the middle of a bunch of buttons. I glance at the dark screen, and my heart starts beating, hard.

There is a baby growing in me, right now. And I'm about to see it.

I smile tremulously at Konstantin, and he opens his mouth to say something, but then the door opens. The tech introduces herself kindly and professionally before walking us through what the appointment will entail. She'll take measurements and photos, then hands us off to the doctor.

I glance over to see Konstantin sitting stiffly in his chair once things get started. Leaning back, the pillow is insanely comfortable and takes my mind off of how cold the ultrasound gel is. The screen looks like a videogame from the nineties, which would be funny if I wasn't so nervous.

A little blob appears. Barely noticeable, and I'm not sure, but...

"Is that... it?" I ask. The tech smiles, her eyes still on the screen as she clicks and rolls.

"Yes. And it looks like you're about seven weeks along... so, a little early to be seen by us, but that's fine. The doctor will tell you when she wants to do the next checkup."

I glance over at Konstantin and then do a double-take. He's staring intently at the screen with an expression I've never seen on his face before.

It's almost... infatuation. But softer.

If *this* is how he feels about our child, then I feel much better about the agreement. I'm suddenly second-guessing my decision to move out west, but if I have to leave my—*our* —baby behind, at least I know that Konstantin will do anything for them.

I'll give you everything. I'll destroy myself, for you.

His words echo in my head. Somehow, I'd tucked them away, even in the throes of passion. Of course I doubted them; they were just something for a man obsessed with fucking a baby into me to say, mindless babble while he plowed into me over and over.

But now...

A strange mixture of elation, sadness, and grief wells up in me as I stare at the screen. The tech explains the measurements she's taking, and she prints a few images for us to take. I hand them to Konstantin, and he stares down at them reverently.

The rest of the appointment goes by in a blur as I try to keep my emotions at bay. Over and over, I have to stop myself from touching my belly, from cradling our child.

When the doctor leaves the room briefly to print out our care sheet, Konstantin grips my thigh with one hand.

"Are you okay?" he asks, eyes boring into mine.

I do everything I can to keep the tears back.

"Yes," I choke out, giving him a watery smile. "I'm fine, just—it's a lot."

He nods, agreeing, his eyes misting over. With what, I wonder? Is he worried? Regretting this? Scared, like I am?

I don't regret this. I know that. But one thought keeps coming back to me over and over... I wish *she* was here.

In the car ride home, we're both silent. I'm lost in thought, but whenever I pop back into the present, I can tell that Konstantin is watching me closely. He has the driver stop at a realty office and he disappears inside for a short time before returning.

Driving through the city, we take a turn and all of a sudden the feeling of things being vaguely familiar coalesces into recognition.

I gasp, covering my mouth, eyes filling and spilling over.

"Audrey." He reaches over, unclicks my seatbelt, and slides me across the backseat to him. I press into his side, ashamed of the tears. "What's wrong?" he murmurs, beard tickling my forehead.

Glancing over his shoulder, out the window, I take in the familiar street—the familiar home.

"I used to live here," I whisper, voice trembling. "With my Nana. That was her house."

Before it went into foreclosure.

Before I had to scramble to find the apartment on

Magnolia, with Sal's help, though now that memory is bitter.

Konstantin's large hand cradles my head against him. I let the tears and the grief come, in waves, soaking into his perfect, bespoke suit. By the time we're out of the city and almost home the feeling of hopelessness has receded.

"Leave us," he tells the driver once we're parked. The man gets out and walks down the street, lighting a cigarette. I wonder what the neighbors must think.

For what feels like a full minute, Konstantin only watches me. I wipe at the damp trails, self-conscious and finally giving in to gently covering my belly with one hand.

"You're alone," he says finally.

I nod. Today has been overwhelming, to say the least.

And if I'm going to do this, I need Konstantin to understand some things about my situation—about how hard this will be for me.

"It's been one year, today, since my grandmother died."

His eyes widen in realization as I continue: "She raised me. And I wasn't ready for her to leave... I didn't realize how sick she was. She was good at hiding it."

I don't need to remind him of my angry, forced confession—that I borrowed the money from Sal and his boss for my Nana's home care. That fear and love are why I'm in this situation.

"And your parents...?"

I shake my head. "My mom, Nell, she's an addict. Always has been. She dropped me off when I was three months old and I've only seen her a handful of times over the years. I have no idea where she is. My father..." I shrug, giving him a hopeless look. I have no idea who my father is.

He nods slowly, taking that information in. Then something occurs to me: "Didn't you, I don't know... do research on me, or anything? Before deciding...?" I gesture at my belly, and Konstantin reaches out, ghosting his fingers over my curves, a small smile on his face.

"No," he admits. "It wouldn't have mattered; I only wanted you. Not your past. Not other's mistakes."

The declaration calms something in me. The grief isn't gone, but it's lessened.

Konstantin carefully unfolds the ultrasound images from his wallet and hands them to me. We bend close, heads over the tiny blob that will be our future.

"My family," he says quietly, almost a whisper, "I lost them, too. My brother... he passed away. After I left Russia." Clearing his throat, he pulls away and looks out the window. I reach out, but stop shy of touching him, not sure if he wants comfort. "My mother didn't want me. Only the money. And, well, it looks like neither of us have a father to blame for our misfortune."

His smile is beautiful and sad all at once.

I can't help myself. I lean forward, practically crawl into his lap, and take his face in my hands. His beard is thick, much darker than his silver hair. For a moment I imagine what a younger, desperate Konstantin would look like, new to America. Fighting for a future.

My lips press against his gently. Konstantin relaxes into the kiss, covering my mouth with his, sucking teasingly on my bottom lip. He squeezes my hip, presses his other hand to my belly.

"You'll never be alone now, Audrey," he murmurs. "You'll always have me, and our child. Always."

148

Chapter 18

Konstantin

"This one."

The curator nods stiffly, jotting something down in his notepad before glancing at Holly, my acquisitions specialist. Her eyes run over the oil painting before us—an abstract, massive, in blues and blacks and greens.

It has stirred something in me that I both long for and hate. It looks like... home. Like the pine forests I used to stare at from the living room window, where Mikhail and I slept on pads on the floor.

The curator thumbs a small red sticker next to the piece and a few guests murmur, surprised or envious. Holly and the man walk away into the depths of the gallery to discuss payment.

Taking a sip of champagne, my eyes scan the room for the artist. I'm curious about her, and how she managed to capture such an evocative memory that has been buried in my mind for decades.

Instead, my gaze locks on someone *else*. Someone very, very familiar.

Giuseppe Sartorre.

His gray hair is slicked back, heavy black glasses resting on an aquiline nose. He's tall and slim aside from the pouch that all Italian men seem to develop later in life, accentuated by the cashmere sweater tucked perfectly into his trousers.

A small group is being entertained by one of Giuseppe's stories. He's a charming man; we've met several times in life, almost always politely. Anything *impolite* between our factions takes place in back alleys, at night, in secret.

Giuseppe glances up and smiles when he sees me watching. His wave is so grandfatherly that I scowl, taking another sip of champagne.

With a word, the crowd around Giuseppe disperses. He strolls casually in my direction, hands in his pockets.

"Konstantin. I would say I'm surprised to see you here, but you've always been a man of good taste."

"Giuseppe. Likewise. Though I didn't strike you as a fan of abstract work."

He shrugs, the cashmere sweater hiding his drooping shoulders. Giuseppe Sartorre, crime boss of the Italian mob, is aging. It's beginning to get noticeable.

My eyes narrow.

"I'm not, really. You know, I prefer more realism. Those old paintings of a table laid with a feast—pheasants, grapes, a cat trying to steal from a saucer of milk." He laughs, and it's a pleasant sound. Maybe in another life a man like Giuseppe and I could've been friends. I'd pay a pretty penny to be able to sit down with him and talk about our experiences; the men we've killed with our bare hands, the insurgents we've had to stifle in our ranks, maybe even the days before we became killers.

"This is more of my son's interest."

He lifts his chin in the direction of the crowded gallery and it's suddenly easier to pick out Davide Sartorre, a gorgeous woman on his arm who must be his wife, Giacomo Sartorre, and Rocco Sartorre.

Rocco, though, is noticeably drunk. And harassing one of the curator's young assistants.

Annoyance flashes across Giuseppe's features. He's an old man now, but if I were Rocco I wouldn't want to be on the receiving end of his father's anger.

I also wouldn't want to be in the running to become the next Don.

"Fia," I comment drily, noticing the absence of his daughter, "she doesn't enjoy art?"

He shrugs. "Fia is finishing up some... *work* for me. In upstate New York." Giuseppe catches the way my face goes flat, and laughs. "Don't worry, Konstantin. We already know all about your warehouse up there; you have no competition from us. My family is from Sicily, we prefer warmer climates. North Carolina, Atlanta, Boca. No, Fia is just hunting down a runner. Getting what we're owed."

I relax, taking in the art once more as our conversation lapses into silence. My thoughts are with Audrey, who I didn't dare bring to this event.

Yes, I made sure that she was very publicly declared *mine*.

But now that she's carrying my child, I don't want to put her in unnecessary danger.

As if reading my mind, Giuseppe casually comments, "I heard you're starting a family. Congratulations."

Immediately, panic, fear and anger balloon in my chest. Glancing toward the street, I have the urge to text Lev—to ask him to make sure that Audrey is safe.

"How do you know?" I ground out, grip tightening on the champagne glass.

"Ah, well. Lucia," he gestures toward Davide's wife, "she has been struggling—please keep this private, Konstantin—for a long time with infertility. I believe she and your... child's mother visit the same clinic." His smile is flat, calm. "I've paid them, of course, to keep me updated on changes to their clientele. Imagine my surprise..."

He trails off, leaving me to roast in my own shame.

I should've thought of that.

I should've requested immediate notification of potential threats, paid the staff off to break HIPAA law and tell me every last detail about every woman's spread legs in that place.

"Take my advice," Giuseppe sighs, "maybe stop at... one. Or two, if you feel you need a contingency plan. But more than that." He shakes his head, watching his children arguing—grown adults almost causing a scene at an art gallery opening.

His admission makes me feel calmer, though not safe. Not anywhere near safe.

I didn't want Giuseppe Sartorre to know about my heir until I was positive I could keep the baby safe. Until Audrey was on her way to the west coast—though my heart aches to think that—and I had security in place.

"Maybe," Giuseppe smiles, "it will make you a more

forgiving man. I've heard what your men did to mine at the Hudson."

The champagne glass shatters in my hand.

Guests nearby pause, a woman gasping in surprise as blood pools and drips from my palm. Holly hurries over, pressing a napkin into my hand, shielding me from as many people as she can.

"Mr. Martynov, do you—"

"I'm fine."

My tone scares her off. She drops her gaze, nods, and disappears. Hopefully to get more napkins. The blood comes fast. This may need stitches.

Clenching my jaw, I slide my phone out of my pocket with one hand and text Lev: **Make sure the physician is at my home by the time I leave.**

He doesn't ask why. It's not his job to.

Giuseppe's eyebrows are raised. Davide looks like he wants to come over, but his wife and Giacomo are talking him down.

Good move. I never imagined I'd take the Sartorre family out so publicly, in an art gallery, but if I have to...

"Calm yourself, Konstantin," Giuseppe murmurs. "It was not a threat. Just a joke. Truly," he speaks quieter, leaning toward me, "I'm happy for you. Family gives your life meaning. And from what I know of you, you've been without family for a long, long time."

I let that sit, squeezing the napkin until it's bloody pulp in my hand. When my pulse steadies and Holly reappears with another stack of napkins, some staff member already on their knees wiping up the blood drops, I finally answer: "My men went after yours, Giuseppe, because yours no longer seem to know where the boundaries lie. Are you bringing on new blood without educating them?"

His face hardens.

There—there's the man who started his empire. Who took over half of this city, gave me a run for my money until I proved myself.

We've had a peaceful few decades, more or less. If my men and I kill it's out of necessity; and it isn't usually a rival group.

But things seem to be changing.

"My men," he says through clenched teeth, "no, those are not *my men*. They are masquerading as loyalists, but Giacomo tells me..." He glances around the room. The guests, recognizing us, know enough to turn away. Not just to pretend not to listen, but to *be sure* they don't listen.

"Giacomo tells me that there is a group pushing back. Skimming from their own." He shakes his head, rage purpling his throat and crawling in an ugly way up toward his face. "I'm trying to avoid an all-out riot, Konstantin, trying to find the bad seed quietly. In the background. But between you and I," our eyes meet. The blood has stopped running, but I can feel my pulse in my palm. "Between you and I, I'm expecting nothing short of an uprising. Soon. So, if your men feel the need to exterminate the rats..."

He shrugs.

I know where we stand now. As much as I feel for Giuseppe, it's a relief to know that he isn't immortal. That he, too, has to put his own dogs down sometimes.

"What are the chances," I ask drily, "that your men would do something so stupid as to pit us against one another? To hope that we take each other out?"

An ugly smile curls Giuseppe's lips. Giacomo, who I sense is the true leader of the three brothers, is watching us intently as Davide and his wife laugh with guests.

"The chances are low," Giuseppe grunts, "but never zero. The man who plans something like that—he would be *uno scemo.*"

A fool.

The gears are turning in my head. In this world, in my dark world, there is no such thing as a coincidence. If tonight is a kind of truce, I decide to take a chance.

"Sal Imperi."

The flash of recognition in Giuseppe's eyes, alone, is enough to confirm it.

"What are the chances that he's a bigger imbecile than I realized when we met?"

Giuseppe nods. "I'd say you have a good sense of people, if you caught onto that. Sal has been oily since the day he started climbing the ranks. Of course," Giuseppe grins, holding a hand out to shake mine, "men like us, you and I, we would never work together... but do whatever you need to. I won't get in your way unless..."

He looks meaningfully toward his boys, his heirs, and there's no further need to explain.

I won't touch any of the Sartorres.

I don't need to. Giuseppe Sartorre has confirmed a suspicion that has been growing like a vine in me for weeks now.

Sal Imperi isn't just the rat—he's the nest.

Chapter 19

Audrey

The knock startles me. It's gentle, barely there, but after the nightmare earlier... I can't help my heart pounding in my chest. Waking up to an empty house in the middle of the day after dreaming of Sal hunting me down wasn't ideal. It took everything in me to resist texting Konstantin...

And I'd failed.

I'm still holding my breath when I open the door, not sure what I expect—another shouting match, another bloody confrontation. Sal's threats still ring in my ears, echoing from every surface of the house after that nightmare. Only this time around, he threatened to cut the baby out of me.

Instead, it's Lev.

And behind him—three more men. All quiet, all enormous. All dressed in charcoal and black, as if the mob has a standard uniform. This gets a smile from me that I try to hide, and Lev quirks an eyebrow.

He doesn't say a word, unsurprisingly. But the others...

they nod at me, one of them giving the smallest smile, as if to say *we're not here to hurt you*. Not unless someone makes us.

"Uh..." I glance behind me, at the house that I'm about to leave because of a silly dream. I mean, it's not like I've never had nightmares before. "Is it... he's fine with this...?"

Lev nods, then takes his phone out, typing effortlessly for a moment. A modulated voice sounds out: "Mr. Martynov would like you to spend the night at his home, Audrey, if you're comfortable with that. He is unfortunately unable to stay here overnight due to a meeting this morning."

It's so professional, so unlike what I imagine Lev would ever speak like, that I just stare for a moment. When I'd texted Konstantin earlier to see if he could come be with me, there was no reply. I didn't expect this.

"Is he mad?"

Lev doesn't answer. Instead, he just gestures.

Come.

I stare at them for another second and then sigh. There's no point in arguing. I don't even change out of the soft cotton lounge dress I fell asleep in after working at the remote office today. I just grab my phone, a cardigan, and my purse.

When I step outside, Lev is already walking, the other men falling in around me like I'm some kind of princess—or prisoner.

It feels excessive. But... sweet. In a twisted, only-Konstantin way.

They're protecting me. *He's* protecting me. I'm not sure I've ever had someone do that, and it finally starts to dawn on me that maybe Konstantin really meant what he said. Maybe there's a world where I don't feel so alone anymore...

Or maybe you're still dreaming, a small voice sounds in my head.

The car is sleek and black, idling beneath the streetlight even though it's not quite dark enough for them yet. No license plate visible. The windows are tinted black, darker than what's legal, but that's never stopped Konstantin before.

The inside smells like leather and cedar and something else. Him, maybe.

I slide into the back seat and let the silence settle around me. The doors click shut. Lev sits across from me in the rear-facing seat, watching me like I might disappear.

I think I fall asleep again—somewhere in the hum of the engine and the rhythm of the road. I'm exhausted, wrung out. The last few days have bled me dry. Turns out growing a baby does that to you—takes every ounce of your energy.

When I wake up, the car has stopped outside of Konstantin's townhouse. Lev gets out, opens my door, and waits.

As I step out onto the sidewalk, hesitating, this suddenly feels even more ridiculous: texting a crime lord about a nightmare.

* * *

"He will arrive shortly. If you need anything, I will be down in the security room. You can use the intercom or text me." That modulated voice again; I watch as Lev turns away, leaving me in the foyer, and heads down to a lower level.

Text him? Obviously he doesn't know about Konstantin's rule—that he be the *only* contact in my phone. Still, it makes sense... if he's going to have Lev watching out for me, practically stalking me, I might as well have the guy's number.

Just in case.

Slipping my shoes off, I wander the townhouse, or at least the floor I'm on, before making my way to the kitchen. The nightmare has worn off as I once again take in the opulence of Konstantin's home. It's exquisite. Nana would have *died* for this kitchen.

She also would've died if she knew who I was dating. Or... sleeping with. Ugh.

The kitchen is gorgeous, but it's lacking something, and I realize what it is right away. There's a sudden, overwhelming urge to *give back,* and even as I begin opening drawers and rummaging around, I mutter to myself: "Must be the hormones. This is ridiculous."

But I find aprons hanging in a closet perfectly flush with the wall, all the ingredients I need, all the tools. Of course, I'm assuming Konstantin has cooks, and they would without a doubt make sure all the necessities were here.

After staring into the massive refrigerator for a few mindless moments, trying to ignore the expensive champagne and the urge to down a glass (not allowed), I juggle some peaches against my belly and let them roll onto the counter.

It's not long before I have the makings for a peach cobbler, and the kitchen looks like a *real* kitchen. And smells like it, thanks to the cinnamon. The oven warms and when it beeps I slide the cobbler in, dust my palms on the apron, and consider cleaning up.

In another surge of emotion, I let out a small, panicky laugh. God, this is so silly. I went from padding accounts for a construction company this morning to hair tied up in a messy bun, barefoot, covered in flour.

Like some kind of Stepford wife who wandered into a mafia hideout.

But I feel safe. Like the nightmare never happened, like *Sal* never happened to me to begin with.

It's terrifying.

And when I hear the door open and the unmistakable sound of Konstantin's footsteps, the click of his heeled boots. My heart doesn't leap in fear.

It... flutters.

When he steps into the kitchen, his eyes catch on mine immediately.

Then drop.

To the apron.

To the bump.

My stomach is just beginning to show, and I cover it self-consciously.

He stops walking, like I've knocked the air out of him.

"Audrey."

It's not a greeting. It's a need.

I swallow, turning back to the counter. "I hope you like cinnamon. I didn't ask. I just... needed to do something. To take my mind off... I'm sorry I texted you," I blurt out. "I think the hormones are affecting my dreams. They're so much more vivid, and I was alone in the house. If this is weird or, Lev said you're busy tomorrow, I can just go home..."

Turning away, I try to ignore the heat of embarrassment on my cheeks.

Home.

He doesn't answer right away. Instead, I feel him behind me. Not touching. Just... looming.

And then his hand is on my hip. Firm. Possessive.

The mess is completely forgotten. I lean into him, my back pressed to his chest.

"I wasn't sure if I'd hear from you," I murmur. "I thought it was silly..."

"It wasn't silly. I didn't want to text." His voice is low. Gravel and silk. "If I could destroy your nightmares, Audrey, I would. You know that?"

I nod, and he presses a kiss to the side of my neck, his beard scraping gently.

"You look... domesticated."

I roll my eyes. "Don't ruin it. Honestly, I'm not much of a baker. I can manage this and maybe chocolate chip cookies."

"No." His hand slides up, pressing flat over my belly. "I mean it."

I close my eyes. The kitchen smells like sugar, but he smells like danger. Like power. Like inevitability. And when he turns me around, when he lifts me onto the counter without a word, I don't protest.

"Maybe," he murmurs, his hands pushing up the apron, the lounge dress, "I can't chase your nightmares away, but maybe I can make you forget them." His mouth finds the curve of my jaw. He kisses me like he owns me—like this was always the plan. And I *want* it.

Konstantin parts my legs and breathes, "I love the way you look like this. Coming home to you, barefoot and..." His hand ghosts over my belly again, settles between my legs, knuckles pressed against my center. "I want you."

I whisper, "Then have me."

Without hesitation, I pull his shirt over his head, only vaguely intrigued that it's a t-shirt and relatively dirty. He smells of salt, sweat, musk, and dirt.

The combination makes me wet.

Not knowing what he's been doing to get so dirty, for his muscles to be so tight as I run my hands over them, *makes me want him.* I want the safety and the danger and the man who sends four armed men to walk me to a car.

His fingers undo the knot of the apron, and it falls to my waist. Another twist, and the button at the back of my neck is undone; mouth devouring mine, Konstantin pulls the dress down my shoulders, exposing my breasts.

They've been heavier lately, uncomfortable, and I flinch involuntarily. His dark eyes find mine, asking me to trust him.

Leaning forward, I give myself to him. Without question.

His hands cup my full breasts, gently, reverently. This isn't the punishing, bruising massage that has turned me on before, the grip that owns me as he bounces me on his cock.

He kisses along my collarbone, his free hand sliding up the skirt of the apron and my dress, fingers hooking into my underwear. I'm so exhausted, foggy, turned on, that all I can do is groan and wriggle as he pulls them down my legs.

The he nudges between my knees.

"You're sure?" I ask, glancing down at my flowered belly and the dirty counter.

Konstantin growls. He doesn't seem to care that the work jeans he has on are about to get powdered, not when he flicks open the button, undoes the zip, and hefts his already hard cock into his hand.

I watch as he pumps it once, twice.

A glistening of precum drools at the tip. The sight makes my pussy clench, and I scoot forward on the counter eagerly, holding onto his shoulders.

Wrapping an arm under my ass, he heaves me up and manages to drop me on his cock in one forceful move. The sensation of being stretched and filled is so unexpected that I gasp, the nightmare disappearing from my mind, nervous system taken over by the surge of pleasure that rushes to my toes and the top of my head.

With a moan, I try to gyrate against him. Konstantin buries his face in my neck and bounces me on his hips, my thick thighs wrapped around him, trembling from the effort and from the toe-curling sensation of being pounded over and over.

"Mine," he murmurs, kissing his way down my tender breasts. "Mine, mine, mine."

It isn't long before I come. All day my body has been exhausted, on edge, nerves wracked, and as his hands grip my ass it's easy to fall over the edge, not even realizing as I mirror back to him: "Yours. *Yours, yours.*"

When it's over, when we both fall against the counter, Konstantin's cum dripping down my thighs, it's all I can do to stay awake.

He realizes and carries me gently to the bedroom, giving me a clean robe to wear. Sitting on the edge of the bed, he pulls up the comforter, then brushes a piece of hair from my face.

"I'll kill him," he says softly.

My eyes snap open. "What?"

"Sal. The moment you say the word."

"I thought you already planned to," I answer drily. Fully aware that I've already asked him once *not* to kill Sal.

His mouth twists. "That was the nightmare, wasn't it? *He* was the nightmare?"

My eyelids feel so heavy, I'm not sure I can keep them open. I nod, hand searching his out under the comforter. In that moment, half asleep, I feel an odd mix of emotions: content; fulfilled; unsure; and like all I want, more than anything, is for him to hold me.

Before I have the time to fear that desire, sleep overtakes me.

Chapter 20

Konstantin

The morning is good.

Too good.

Sunlight slices through the slats of the blackout curtains in my bedroom, scattering against hardwood floors. The townhouse is silent. Still. Not even Lev pacing on the floor below.

And Audrey is here.

She's asleep on her side, breath feathering out softly, the duvet kicked down to her waist. Her robe is loose, the curve of her belly just visible beneath the fabric. My child is in there. Mine.

The sight of her like this—peaceful, trusting, soft— rattles me in a way no war, no deal, no death has ever managed. I should be at the Spire right now, overlooking transactions that rake in more in a day than most people will see in their lives. I should be putting out fires, issuing threats, reviewing new contracts.

Instead, I'm standing here like a man who's lost.

A man who's found something he was never meant to have.

Something he doesn't know how to keep.

You wanted this, I remind myself. Is that true, though? Did I want *this?*

What I wanted was an heir. A reason to keep going. When Audrey gave me her stipulation, that I let her go after the birth, I agreed.

But now...

I tear myself away.

Downstairs, my boots thud heavily against the tile as I shove them on. I ignore breakfast, ignore Lev's usual offer of a brief, and tell him to get her home. I leave the townhouse and let the autumn air bite at my skin. Cold is good. It keeps me sharp.

The construction site is already humming by the time I get there. Generators buzz. Jackhammers thunder against concrete. The smell of metal and sweat and earth fills my lungs. I roll up my sleeves, grab a pair of gloves, and take a sledgehammer from one of the men.

No one asks questions. No one dares.

Despite everything I've done to build this empire, the most satisfying work for me is often the actual *building.* Not watching numbers rack up in the accounts; but watching men struggle, make a living, earn their lives.

When their boss shows up in steel-toed boots instead of Italian leather, it's because he needs the pain. The distraction. The weight of something in his hands that isn't her.

* * *

I don't think of Audrey at first.

I slam the hammer down again and again, pounding rebar and ego beneath the blows. I lose track of time. The sun climbs. My back aches, my shirt sticks to my skin. It's only when one of the foremen calls for a break that I stop.

That's when I see him.

A small boy. Six, maybe seven. Standing beside one of the men I recognize—Aleksy, a welder with twenty years in. The boy has dark hair, cut unevenly, and big brown eyes that take in everything. He's holding a sandwich in one hand and a toy truck in the other.

Something about him coils around my ribs and squeezes.

He looks too much like Mikhail.

My little brother was thin as a rail. Always hungry, always smiling. He had a way of making a game out of nothing; one time, I brought him home a dented metal truck someone had thrown out. He treated it like it was made of gold. I watched him fall asleep with it clutched to his chest.

And then I left.

I told him I'd be back. I promised him America would change everything, even our mother—she'd be kinder, I'd whispered. She'd be able to love us.

I didn't get the chance to return in time.

Mikhail had died the winter after I left. Pneumonia. No medicine, despite the money I was sending back. Nothing like what I would eventually be able to send, but it was more than anything she—or her boyfriends—ever made. Should have been more than enough for Mikhail to be seen at the hospital if she'd cared enough to take him.

She said it like she was ordering groceries. Like my brother's life was just one more debt she didn't want to pay.

I nod to the boy.

Aleksy notices. "This is Emil," he says, pride in his voice. "My youngest. The school called in a half day." The flick of his eyes to his boy, the large hand on Emil's shoulder —I understand easily that as proud as Aleksy is, he's nervous.

I have a reputation, after all.

Crouching beside the boy, I offer him a piece of rebar, like a sword. He beams at me and takes it in both hands.

For a second, I imagine a different life. One where Mikhail made it, where I went back in time. One where we both lived like kings..

I leave the site late in the afternoon, after making sure Aleksy gets an envelope for his boy. Inside: tuition for the next three years, and a card with a number he can call if anything ever happens to his family.

"Anything," I say.

Aleksy nods, eyes misting. "Yes, sir."

But instead of going back to the townhouse, I go to her place. *Our place,* the voice whispers, and I try to shake it off, not wanting to think about what it means—that I think of that country house as a home. As somewhere I belong.

I don't park directly outside but pull around the corner and walk.

Old habits. Ones I can't seem to break now that I know there's something more, something hidden, happening in the city. I haven't forgotten Giuseppe's blessing, or his warning; somewhere, someone is trying to take him down.

And it seems they're testing my territory as well to pit us against one another. I wonder if they've found out that the two most dangerous men in the city know.

Through the diamond-paned window, I see her silhouette on the couch. She's curled on her side, a blanket pulled up, the TV casting a soft glow across her face.

She's asleep again, exhausted no doubt. I take a twisted pleasure in that: she wants to work, wants to be useful, but I wonder how long that will really last. The pregnancy is draining her, our child growing strong. It makes me want to carry her everywhere. To wrap her up in cashmere and seal the doors and make sure nothing ever touches her again.

I should go inside.

But I don't.

I stand in the shadows and watch her.

Like a fucking *podonok,* a creep.

But a reverent one.

She shifts, murmurs something in her sleep, then stills.

That's how Lev finds me. I hear him approach before I see him. His tread is familiar. Purposeful.

"How has she been?"

He types quickly, flashes the screen in my direction instead of using the audio. **Fine. Sleeping mostly. Left the office early.**

Movement flashes behind the window. Kashmere; she's here late, walking the house. She looks innocent, like someone's mother, like a maid. Only I and a few other, including Olena, know that Kashmere has killed her fair share of men to get where she is.

169

Which is why I have her watching the mother of my child.

"Why are you still here?"

Lev pauses. I don't like that.

This time, he concentrates on his words before turning the phone toward me. **I was going to check on the perimeter. But it looks like I'm not the only one who had that idea.**

Meeting his gaze, I don't break eye contact. He knows what I want; he knows that *I* know that something is off.

She was followed, he adds quickly. **From the office.**

The blood in my veins turns to ice.

Lev gestures toward the cars up the street, but I don't want to move. It takes Kashmere glancing toward us quickly, trying to mask a look of exasperation, for me to move away from the window. At the edge of the yard, Lev's phone sounds out: **We caught him two blocks from here. Alone. Unarmed. Stupid. Definitely not one of Sartorre's top men—just some kid. I think they're probing. Seeing how easy she'd be to grab.**

I inhale slowly, evenly.

"And now?"

He's in a bag. Probably halfway down the Hudson.

I nod once.

"Good," I say. "But next time? Kill them sooner."

The kid shouldn't have even made it this far. I stride slowly back to the window. Audrey stirs again, pressing her hand to her stomach in her sleep.

A protective gesture.

I wonder if the baby knows. If it feels that. An ache forms in my chest; did my mother curve a hand over her belly like that? Something in me doubts it. And then another thought follows quickly after: How can I make sure the baby knows that it's protected by *me*? That I'll protect them both?

"More men," I say. "Discreet. But everywhere. Cameras too. Inside and out."

Lev nods.

"If anything happens to her..."

His silence is absolute. He understands. It doesn't matter that he's led my men for years now, that I'd trust him with my life.

If he loses hers...

"If anything happens to her or the child," I continue, voice low and lethal, "burn the city down. I want them all dead. Italians, allies, messengers, middlemen. I don't care. I want them erased."

Lev bows his head.

He knows I mean it.

Later, when I go inside, finally released from the fear that froze me in place, I don't feel powerful.

I feel terrified.

She's still asleep, lips parted, blanket slipped low. Her laptop is closed on the coffee table. A half-empty glass of water rests beside it. The soft scent of vanilla and clean cotton hangs in the air thanks to Kashmere.

And I am utterly ruined.

I kneel beside Audrey, careful not to wake her, and press my palm to the slight swell of her belly.

My child.

My blood.

I didn't think I wanted a family.

I thought I wanted control.

But this?

This is the only thing that's ever felt real.

Chapter 21

Audrey

Three months in, and I still don't want to know the gender, even though they've offered several times at my appointment the other day. Konstantin hadn't argued. He didn't even blink. Just looked up from the page he was signing, nodded, and muttered something like, "Makes no difference. It's mine."

The calm in his voice made me pause. I thought a man like him—so focused on legacy—would demand a son. An heir. I thought he'd already picked out a name, a school, a future.

But he didn't care. He just wanted the baby.

And when, alone in the car, he pressed a strangely chaste kiss to my lips, it made me think he might want me, too.

I hate the Spire.

173

It's beautiful, polished, deadly. Every floor is clinically perfect. But now that I don't need to be there every day, I can see it for what it is: a warehouse of risk. Maybe it's the maternal instinct kicking in, but the last thing I want is to be seen entering those doors. So, when I step into the elevator this afternoon, stomach tight under the silk blouse I'll have to forsake soon, I can already feel the pressure climbing up my spine.

Chrissy had offered to run the errand for me—some transfer documents that needed Konstantin's signature—but I didn't want her walking into the lion's den. Especially not when I've seen how Lev watches her. I'm not sure if something's there, but... either way, I'd like to keep her off their radar. She's the only friend I have, and the only one I can confide in about my situation.

Better if *I* see him, even if it leaves my heart pounding in my throat and my thighs pressed too tightly together.

The elevator chimes softly on the 28th floor.

I step out.

And I freeze.

Konstantin is standing just outside the glass office doors. Not unusual. He does that sometimes—paces while he's on the phone, gaze distant, hands in his pockets.

But this time... he's not alone.

Olena.

There's something about how they're standing that feels... intimate. The cock of her thin hips, hand on her waist, draws attention to how feminine she is under all that intimidation. Olena is a beautiful woman in a harsh way— I've always known that, but now I'm seeing it in a whole different light as she leans into him, speaking quietly.

Konstantin is saying something in Russian. Too low for me to catch. But whatever it is—it makes her smile in that quiet, intimate way that makes it feel like it's just the two of them. There are rumors about Olena, plenty of them, but all of a sudden I'm wondering... is it possible to work so closely together and not have some kind of deep emotional connection?

Possible to kill together, rely on one another, build an empire together... a knot of jealousy burns in my sternum.

This is different than how I've contributed to Martynov Global Holdings for the past year and a half. Olena has literally *killed* for him. Has he done the same for her?

Is that why she's so loyal? Or is it something else?

I shouldn't care.

I have no right to care. After all, I'm just the surrogate.

I watch for another second—maybe two—and then push the glass door open harder than necessary. The sound makes both of them look over.

Olena's eyes narrow.

Konstantin straightens.

His eyes drag over me slowly—bare legs, rounded belly, blouse too snug, lips pressed into a tight line.

"Miss Wolfe," he says, his voice all quiet thunder. "How fortunate. We were just speaking of you."

I arch a brow. "Oh?"

Olena steps back slightly, arms crossing. I can't tell if she's uncomfortable or annoyed. I don't care at the moment, but judging from past interactions, she does *not* approve of the use that Konstantin has put me to.

"Your file was needed for the Avenue development

review," Konstantin explains. "Olena mentioned you flagged a discrepancy."

"Oh," I say lightly. "So *that's* what you two were giggling about?"

Giggling. I wince inwardly. I sound like a jealous housewife.

Konstantin's lip twitches. "Is something wrong, Miss Wolfe?"

"No, nothing." I step forward, placing the manila folder on the edge of his desk. "Though you might want to wipe the lip print off your shirt."

Am I losing my mind? Olena's eyes flash. She's *not* wearing lipstick, never does, but I can't seem to stop myself. There truly is a red smudge, *just there.*

His brow lifts. "Excuse me?"

"Right there," I say, pointing to his collar. "Unless that's blood. I forget—it's hard to tell with you."

He chuckles, and Olena's lips quirk up in a smile. Before he can say more, I pivot toward the door. But he follows.

"Audrey."

I pause, his breath brushing my neck.

"You're jealous."

"I'm not."

He leans in closer. "You are."

I turn, trying to glare at him but failing. The sight of his smirk—infuriating and smug—makes my stomach flutter and my throat tighten. Olena slips past the two of us, her eyes sliding from one to the other.

"You're at work," she reminds him, her accented voice somehow severe and gorgeous all at once. "Keep that in mind, Martynov. Wouldn't want anyone to see you... vulnerable."

Then she's gone. And I'm left to face Konstantin's accusation.

"It's the hormones," I say flatly.

"Of course," he agrees. "Pregnancy does strange things to women. Makes them territorial. Possessive. Sometimes they want to... *claim* their mate."

My face heats. "You're not a wolf, Konstantin."

"No." His gaze drops to my belly. "But you are, *malen'kiy volk.*"

"Don't say it like that."

"Why not? You're the one snarling at poor Olena. Who, by the way..." he adds, brushing a thumb under my chin, "prefers women."

I blink. "She does?"

He nods, and his grin turns downright wicked. "She prefers *brunettes*, actually. You should be careful."

"You're an asshole."

"Yes," he says shortly.

My hand twitches. I want to slap him. Or kiss him. Possibly both.

"Don't you have an empire to run?"

He sighs. "Yes. But you make it very difficult to focus when you come in smelling like citrus and bad intentions. Did you really need to see me, little wolf, or were you just looking for an excuse? Is there something I can..." his fingers drag down my side, "...do for you?"

I ignore that and turn on my heel.

Behind me, I hear him murmur something in Russian again—something amused and low—and I nearly trip as I leave his office, jaw tight, chest full of fury and something else I can't name.

Possessive. That's what he said.

He's not wrong. I hated seeing him close to someone else. I hated the idea that Olena, of all people, could be close to him in ways I can't. At this moment, in a storm of emotion, I'm both thrilled by his words and very, very aware of the gulf between us.

Konstantin Martynov comes from a different world. He's unknowable, no matter how many nights he spends by my side. No matter how many times he's claimed me as his.

* * *

Chrissy's waiting by the elevators.

She gives me a look, eyes bouncing between me and the closed office door. "You okay?"

I lie, embarrassed at the truth. "Fine."

She hesitates. "You know you don't have to pretend around me, right? With Mr. Martynov making it obvious that you two are..."

I wait for her to finish, a tired smile on my face, but she grasps for words desperately. Nods at my belly. As awkward as this is, I can tell by the twinkle in her eye that she's also excited for me.

"I'm not. Pretending, I mean. Sorry Chris—I'm just tired. This," I gesture at my ever-swelling belly, "is pretty exhausting. Just a warning."

She tilts her head. "Right. I'm two double shifts away from accidentally laundering a mafia slush fund."

I stare at her.

She sighs. "That wasn't a joke."

My stomach drops. "What?"

Chrissy glances around. The hallway's quiet. Lev's nowhere in sight. She grabs my arm and pulls me closer.

"I found something, Aud. Something *bad*. Someone's been accessing accounts they shouldn't be in. High-level stuff—stuff even I don't have clearance for. It's subtle, but I noticed a few flags while I was reconciling the Petrovia spreadsheet."

My skin goes cold.

"Petrovia's under lock and key," I whisper.

"Exactly. *I'm* the only one with access. And trust me, I got a good talking to when they assigned it to me about what would happen if anyone else were to find out about it. Which is why... I'm scared," she admits, voice dipping into a whisper.

"And this... this couldn't just be a mistake?"

"No. It's too clean. Too specific." Chrissy's voice lowers. "I think someone's trying to siphon off top-level numbers. Not skimming, not laundering. Just... looking. Quietly. Trying to map the structure."

Sal.

God, it has to be Sal.

This is exactly his style—sly, slippery, one step away from implosion. If he's already exhausted me for the fifty grand and realized he can't use me anymore, this is how he'd creep in. By the end, before Duscha gave me up, he was starting to ask me about the Operations Room. About whether or not I had access to their files.

I didn't, but never even got the chance to explain that. If Sal thought that was his way in, he must be digging around another way now. And the Petrovia file might get him there. It's the one thing that tracks where all of Konstantin's money related to *violence* goes.

There's no other way to put it—every item in that spreadsheet has the potential to end lives. Dozens. Thousands even, if things get that bad.

Another mole. Another point of access.

I rub at my temples. "Shit."

"Yeah," Chrissy says. "Shit."

"Okay. I'll bring it up with him."

"Who?"

I look up. "Konstantin."

Her eyes widen. "You're serious?"

"I said I'd tell him if anything else came up. This counts." I glance toward the elevator. "Besides, I can tell you're worried about it. I don't *think* he'd do anything to you, but... just to make sure."

I don't say it, but the words *he's protecting me now* echo quietly in the back of my mind. I wonder how much I could ask of him. *I'll give you everything*—that's what he told me the night he found out I was pregnant. Yes, it was in a post-sex haze, but... did he mean it?

As Chrissy gives me one last squeeze and disappears into the bathroom, I punch the elevator button and step inside when it dings.

The ride down is slow. Nausea twists in my stomach—not from the pregnancy, but from everything else.

I'll tell him tonight. I have to. He said he'd stop by the house after dinner with some associates. If I'm lucky, he'll already be in a good mood.

If I'm *really* lucky, he'll touch me again.

Maybe kiss me.

Maybe claim me the way I want him to.

I press my hand to the slight swell of my belly.

I'm beginning to realize, as I slip into the car that'll take me home, that I might just do anything for Konstantin Martynov—leader of the Russian mafia.

Chapter 22

Konstantin

I've had blood on my hands since before sunrise. I didn't flinch when Olena told me they found Yuri and Sava face-down in a meat locker on the edge of Little Italy. It was a warning—a stupid one, because you don't leave evidence unless you want someone to come knocking. And I will. I'll knock down every door until I find the men who have been harassing mine, whether Giuseppe Sartorre was telling the truth or not.

But not tonight.

Tonight, I have another problem. One who thinks she can issue commands like she's one of my lieutenants. One who has proven herself to be quite *jealous* of my lieutenants.

Audrey showing up at the office and crackling with energy was an amusing distraction after a morning of losses. But it took more effort than I like to admit to mask my frustration and rage.

Sava had a daughter and a stepson. Yuri just came over a month prior, as a favor to a friend. I'd paid for my ticket myself, and now I'd be paying for both of their funerals.

My jaw is tight as I step out of the car in front of the country house. I've been spending more and more time here, and tonight, for the first time in a while, it doesn't feel welcoming. It feels like I'll have to walk in lying through my teeth.

Hiding how truly violent my life is from her.

When I left the Spire half an hour ago, I was so wrathful that I told Lev to stay. To command the men, and make sure they went out ready—for whatever, whoever, was hiding in the shadows. That's why I wasn't alarmed when Audrey texted me, **We need to talk. Tonight.**

She should be grateful I'm showing up at all tonight, after the week I've had. After burying two bodies and tightening the perimeter around the Spire. After Olena confirmed there's someone inside still trying to feed intel to the Italians.

Which is why I'm going to lose it if she starts talking about feelings. My patience has finally run out, and I don't have time to reassure my little wolf. The first priority is keeping her safe; keeping her satisfied will have to come later.

I knock once. Not because I have to. Because I still believe in manners.

The door opens, and for a moment I forget the ache in my jaw.

Audrey's wearing a t-shirt and leggings, hair up in a messy bun that leaves her neck exposed. It's an uncharacteristic look for her, so casual that it catches me off guard. Her eyes widen when she sees me and then narrow.

"You're late."

"I didn't realize I was on your payroll," I growl.

"You're not. But you're on my clock, considering what I found this morning."

Her voice is sharp, her body bristling with energy. She steps aside to let me in, and when I see who's waiting on the other side, I realize that this is definitely not about Olena.

Chrissy.

She's sitting on the couch, her legs curled under her, holding a glass of wine that she clearly regrets pouring the moment I step inside. She's practically vibrating with anxiety.

"This isn't a good time for guests," I mutter.

"She's not a guest," Audrey snaps. "She found the same anomaly I did." She crosses her arms and it's easy to see how cute she'll look when she's angry and *very* pregnant. For a moment, that thought takes the edge off.

I shoot a look at Chrissy, who just gives me a tight nod. Smart. She knows she's in over her head, but she's not stupid.

"Mr. Martynov. I'm sorry to—" she glances at Audrey, then back at me, "interrupt your night."

Ahh. So, she knows we're sleeping together.

A dark, possessive voice snarls in my mind: *But does she know just how deeply entwined Audrey and I are? That I won't let her go unless her roots are ripped from my veins?*

Chrissy bites her lip, so Audrey talks instead: "We think Sal was after more than just the money."

I blink. That name tastes like bile.

"Go on," I say, voice low.

Audrey gestures for Chrissy to speak. Her friend swallows.

"There's been a string of low-level pings in the system. Not from the outside. Not from an external hack. This is someone inside the firewall, using clearance codes that only a handful of us should have. They've been in the Petrovia file, Mr. Martynov."

My brows rise as I drop into an armchair across from the couch. Audrey curls up next to Chrissy, putting a consoling hand on her friend's back. Chrissy swallows down another gulp of wine, her eyes flitting to mine and then away.

She's nervous but not lying.

I glance at Audrey. "So, Sal wasn't just in it for the money. And he wasn't just upset that you've let me possess you."

Chrissy's cheeks go pink at my frank claim. A fire lights in Audrey's eyes—one that, I'm sure if we were alone, she'd let me smother by putting her under me.

"He wanted the keys," she says. "Not the vault. The money was bait. The accounts... how you fund everything, Konstantin... that's what he really wanted. Sal knows now how to bring down your operations from the ground up."

That name on her lips makes something inside me snap taut. I move closer, lowering my voice as I lean over her, hands braced on the back of the couch.

"You could have told me this sooner."

"I didn't know. I swear. I thought he just wanted the money."

"You think I need proof to burn someone alive?"

Chrissy makes a quiet noise and stands.

"I should go."

"Yes," I say.

Audrey gives me a glare but doesn't stop her friend. They murmur quietly to one another, a familiar rhythm to the quiet conversation that I can read from here: Chrissy regrets telling me. Or at least, being in the middle of Audrey and I. Audrey is reassuring her. Chrissy is scared anyway.

As she should be.

I'm not known for forgiving mistakes, and Chrissy letting someone get into the Petrovia file is a mistake.

Once the door clicks shut behind the accountant, I let the silence stretch

Audrey looks at me, jaw tight, matching me inch for inch.

"Sal started asking questions about the Spire right after I borrowed the money. Not just about what I did, but who I reported to. What systems I had access to. He made it seem like he just wanted the money, but..."

"He wanted intel."

She nods. "I think he was a middleman."

I watch her closely, trying to gauge just how much she knows versus how much she suspects. " "You think this has something to do with Giuseppe."

Audrey doesn't flinch at the name. Brave, this one.

"It doesn't."

"...How do you know?"

She doesn't move from the doorway between the foyer and the living room. She's tense, holding her body as if she's expecting Sal to appear at any moment; as if she's back in his destructive, manipulative path.

It's clear how much her Nana meant to her. I can't

imagine losing someone who raised and truly loved you, only to be taken advantage of in the throes of grief.

She crosses to the kitchen and pours herself water. Her hands are shaking. She's trying to hide it, but I see everything.

"Why didn't you tell me he was pressuring you?"

Audrey scoffs. "Before all of..." she gestures between us, at her belly, "this? Because I didn't want to be a pawn again. I wanted to fix it, and I thought he'd stop when he got his money back."

"You can't fix what you don't control."

She turns. "I did control it. That's why I let Duscha catch me."

The words land like a slap.

"What?"

Audrey takes a breath. "I knew Duscha hated me. She didn't exactly hide it, Konstantin. I knew she was watching me like a hawk. So, I stopped hiding the mistakes. I left the line items exposed. I let her find it. Because I knew she'd go straight to you."

I stare at her.

"You wanted me to catch you."

She nods, and I want to laugh, smirk, kiss her until she can't breathe. Instead, the careful mask I've perfected over the years slips over my features: I feel it, as if it's a real thing. Audrey's eyes search my face.

"I know it was suicide, but I needed a way out. Sal wouldn't let me quit. He wanted more access. He wanted everything. The only way out was through."

I can't believe what I'm hearing.

"So, you played me."

"I trusted you," she says. "Even then. That you'd know what to do."

The silence between us turns into something dangerous. My fists clench.

I want to shake her. I want to kiss her. I want to scream.

Instead, I stalk to the window and stare out at the streetlights. "I lost two men this morning," I say, without turning.

She says nothing.

"Yuri and Sava. Killed in a cooler. Died slow."

When I finally glance back, her face is pale.

"That's what I was dealing with when Olena came into my office. Not that I owe you that explanation."

Audrey doesn't blink. "You think... Sal...?"

"I'm beginning to think I underestimated him. A deadly mistake, in my position, but when I met you Audrey—when all I knew was that you owed a debt to him... I thought it was jealousy motivating him. Now, I think he's out for more."

"But wouldn't that mean that Giuseppe Sartorre...?" Her eyes widen in fear. "Are they trying to take you out?" she practically whispers, rushing to my side and getting on her knees. Her hands on my thighs are warm, a buoy in this dark night.

"No. I spoke with Giuseppe a few nights ago. He made it clear—Audrey, you cannot tell anyone else this." Her eyes promise me she won't. "He made it clear that there is some kind of coup in his family, a group that has splintered off. They're trying to pit us against one another. If it's Sal—"

"And he found the Petrovia files," she breathes out. "I thought he was crazy when he threatened you, but with that information could he...?"

"He could. If I hadn't caught him."

For several long moments we sit in silence, my large hands covering Audrey's. Her belly is pressed against my legs, and I feel a slight pressure, a slight flutter. Our eyes meet and she smiles. "The baby."

All of a sudden I'm no longer drowning. I press my hand to the spot, waiting—and then it comes again.

A small kick.

I close the space between us, joining her and kneeling on the decadent rug. My hands gather her close. Our faces are inches apart.

"You still owe them money?"

Shame flashes across her face. She nods. "Yes. With interest."

When her chin drops, I lift it back up with a finger. "Don't be ashamed," I murmur. "We all do what we have to in order to survive."

Her breath catches. Her pupils dilate. The air turns molten.

But I don't touch her.

I rock back, stand, and pull my phone from my coat.

Giuseppe won't answer. But he'll see the message. He always does.

Audrey Wolfe. Her debt with you is cleared. The money will be in your account tomorrow morning.

Then I swipe to my private ledger. The one no one else touches. Not even Olena.

It takes fifteen seconds to transfer thirty thousand to a laundering route we both use. An old truce. One I'm about to break.

It takes another ten seconds to kill the trail. Sal will see the money, think Giuseppe covered his ass. And I'll know she's free.

Holding a hand out, I help her rise to her feet and give her a slow, patient kiss. Audrey leans into it, body melding against mine. Once again I'm tempted to forget everything, take her upstairs, lose myself in her and our future.

"Do you trust me?" she whispers, vulnerable, against my chest.

"Yes."

Her phone on the coffee table lights up. An unknown number flashes a message on the screen: **The balance is zero.**

"What did you just do?" She looks up at me quickly, the phone trembling in her hand.

"Tied off a loose end."

Audrey opens her mouth to press, but I stop her with a look. Not a threat. A promise.

"You told me everything tonight. So let me do what I do best."

She hesitates, then nods.

Outside, a siren echoes in the distance. I step toward the door. Before I open it, I glance over my shoulder.

"If Sal comes near you again, I'll make him wish he was the one who died in that meat locker."

And I mean it.

Chapter 23

Audrey

There's something... *off* when the landlord calls. His voice is clipped as he asks, "It's Aubrey Wolfe, right?"

"Um, Audrey, but... Yes?" Maybe this is just the tone of someone trying to remember which tenant left without giving notice. I still feel bad about that; it's something my mother would have done, ditching an apartment and disappearing, like the many times she left *me*. It's something my Nana would've given me a disapproving look for.

"There's... something for you here. At your old place. It looks like a delivery."

"Oh, is it a package, or--?"

There's a garbled sound on the other end. Then the call drops. I pull back and stare down at my cell. Strange, but then Konstantin must've forgotten to have someone leave a forwarding address.

It must be one of the many baby-related things I've been ordering during this bout of insomnia. I can't even remember what I've added to my cart in the past two weeks, foggy and browsing "Must Haves for New Moms!" articles at 3 a.m. I must have forgotten to change my delivery address on the website.

"Kashmere?" I call out, padding from the sunroom into the kitchen. It's late in the day, but her car is still in the driveway. Ever since the nightmare, Konstantin has asked her to stay over when she can. If not her, I always know the men are out there... somewhere. Sometimes I can see them parked down the street, other times there's just the suggestion of cigarette smoke in the cold air.

The leaves outside rustle and clatter with a breeze. The trees are mostly past turning now, with only a few days of that pretty gold-red-orange coloring before they turn brown.

A shiver goes down my spine.

Then I see Kashmere's keys on the little entryway table.

If I ask to take her car, I'll just get us both in trouble again.

But if she doesn't *know* I'm taking the car, she's off the hook, right?

It's not that long of a drive to the old apartment building on Magnolia, and I'll just have to pop into the mail room on the first floor. If she's cleaning upstairs or assembling something in the nursery, chances are she won't even notice I'm gone.

Frozen with indecision, I stare out the narrow windows on either side of the front door. There, at the edge of the hedgerow near the drive, is a scuff mark. Small, maybe nothing, but fresh—the kind that comes from shoes dragged through gravel. The gravel bed was designed to be uniform, decorative. Someone has disturbed it.

I step closer to the front window.

Then footsteps sound from upstairs, followed by Kashmere's humming.

I palm the keys, slip into the comfortable house slippers that Konstantin had sent over, and carefully open and close the door.

It's *cold* out now that autumn is starting to shift into winter, and even with the heat that this baby is generating, I end up murmuring, "Should've grabbed a coat."

As soon as I slide into the driver's seat and put the key in the ignition, my stomach twists with... what? Not morning sickness which, by the way, I wish someone would've warned me is *not* just reserved for mornings.

Guilt for knowing that I shouldn't be slipping out, alone, like this?

It's a deeper feeling though, a tremor. Kind of like intuition... before I can pin it down, my eyes catch sight of something on the shed.

A dark maroon smear.

...Blood?

"You're losing it," I whisper to myself, fumbling my cell phone. I could call Konstantin right now, or text Lev. But if I do that I definitely won't be able to run out to the apartment.

And I've been feeling so claustrophobic lately—only going back and forth between the house and the satellite office on the edges of the city. I miss Sottovoce. I miss the cafes, the library. It suddenly hits me that as much as I love being Konstantin's, there are people and places from my life *before* him that I miss, badly.

Squaring my shoulders, I decide to run out. It'll be quick. And just to be safe—I shoot Chrissy a text: **Hey,**

you didn't send a package to my old place, did you?

Um, no? she texts back. **Those pregnancy memory issues starting to kick in? How can I forget that gorgeous house your mob boss lover got you?**

Rolling my eyes, I start the car—thankfully, it's a hybrid, quiet and sleek—and back out.

* * *

In less than half an hour, I reach Magnolia Street and park about a block down, staring at my old building.

I haven't stepped foot on these sidewalks since the night Sal tried to strangle me.

Since the first time Konstantin made me feel *safe*.

There's a little fluttery feeling in my belly, and I press a hand there. It reminds me that I'm not just living for myself anymore. And, yeah, after today I need to set down some ultimatums with Konstantin.

I want to see Chrissy more, go check out a book and chat with Emil—who will be shocked I'm pregnant, ugh—maybe go to my Nana's grave.

A sadness sweeps over me like the frigid breeze, but it's gone quick, replaced by determination. Tonight, I'll grab my package (what are the chances it's a "Mafia Nepo Baby" onesie ordered in a state of humorous delirium?), go home and hopefully pass out, get up eight times to pee in the middle of the night, and start fresh tomorrow.

Find meaning outside of being Konstantin Martynov's surrogate.

Begin reclaiming my life.

Smiling softly to myself, I gather my things. Oversized sweater, a purse that I'd downsized since Konstantin insisted I carry a new security-coded wallet instead of cash. I'm halfway across the street when that uneasy feeling scoops out my belly again.

Frozen, I stare up at the floor I used to live on. It seems so long ago now.

A car honks, and I rush the rest of the way to the front door.

Trying to ward off the strange feeling, I text Chrissy again: **Weird to be back on Magnolia.**

Her reply comes almost instantly: **What? What are you doing there, Aud?**

Don't worry. Just picking up a package.

The building looks the same. Beige paint flaking off siding, cheap evergreens in decorative planters out front. Inside the atrium is at least blasting heat from an old vent, and the mailbox is still labeled "Wolfe" in faded Sharpie. There are a few packages piled in the corner, and I bend over as well as I can, shifting them to read the names.

None of which are mine.

I hesitate, phone still in hand, and it buzzes again—like a warning.

Why would you send a package to your old apartment, Audrey?

It's a good question. One that makes my stomach roil again with nerves.

Does Konstantin know you're there?

I tap the message box, thumb poised to type.

That's when I see him.

Sal.

He's leaning against the doorframe like he still belongs there. Like nothing ever changed.

"Audrey."

His voice is cool, melodic, with that New Yorker accent. It's no different than it ever was, but now it makes me feel nauseous.

Two men that I don't recognize flank him. One is wiry and jittery, like he needs a fix. The other looks like he's just stepped out of Rikers, all muscles and aggression in a wife-beater that strains over his frame.

My feet refuse to move.

Sal smiles, slow and oily. "Hey there, *piccola*. You look... rounder."

I flinch. Instinctively, my hand goes to my belly.

"You're not supposed to be here," I say, even though it sounds childish the moment it leaves my mouth. "Konstantin—he had the cops put in an order—"

"Oh?" Sal cocks his head. "But this is where we started. You remember? That shitty futon, the pizza boxes, all those nights I took care of you when you were too sad to do anything else. Crying and crying after the old lady died. Remember when you were almost catatonic after selling her shitty little house?" His grin is feral, cruel. "I figured we could have a little reunion."

My pulse screams danger. Every nerve ending in my body is lit up.

"Go to hell."

"That's not very polite," he replies, stepping forward.

My eyes search the tiny mail room, then the hallway behind Sal. His grin widens. "Oh, no one will come down here, love. There's another guy watching the elevators. And, well…" He glances over his shoulder. I suddenly notice a boot twisted strangely on the ground… attached to a leg… "Your old landlord, he's not in any state to help you right now."

Oh, God.

The call. The strained tone to the landlord's voice. It wasn't annoyance; it was fear. Sal had threatened him into luring me here.

The two men box me in. There's no door behind me, and the tiny windows in this room are frosted. No one outside will see what happens to me here.

And just like that, I realize what this is.

A trap.

Sal's eyes drop to my stomach, and something dark flickers there. Jealousy? Possession? I can't tell anymore. Once, I worried that sleeping with Sal would result in a pregnancy, and I knew that he'd insist I "take care of it." How far I've come, with a man now who would do anything to protect me.

If only he knew where I was.

If only I'd asked Konstantin for a ride or let him know I was heading here.

Sal reaches inside his jacket and pulls out something shiny.

A switchblade.

My breath catches.

"Sal, don't—"

"Don't what? Don't ask questions? Don't point out how you sold me out to the Russians after I made you? After I paid for your Nana's care? After I—"

"You tried to kill me," I snap.

"Because you *owed* me," he snarls. "And I told you there was a price for crossing me." His eyes gleam. "But you know the best part of this little homecoming?"

He pulls something from his back pocket. A piece of paper. Crumpled. It lands at my feet.

I stare at it, not moving.

"Your debt's paid," he says. "Every damn cent. One of Konstantin's dogs wired it directly to my people."

The balance is zero.

That anonymous text I got a few days ago, when Konstantin paid off my debt.

"You're free," he says mockingly. "From me. From all of it. Except one thing."

I look up, wide-eyed.

"You still fucked me over, Audrey. They know I was in the Petrovia files, and *I* know you had something to do with them finding out. You made me look weak. You think the Italians are gonna let that slide?"

My voice cracks. "I thought... you were trying to take Giuseppe's place."

One of the thugs laughs low. Sal looks like I slapped him. Then anger washes over his face.

"Who the *fuck* told you that?" He strides forward, grabs my chin, his fingers bruising my jaw as he puts pressure on. "Shut your God damn mouth."

So, it's true. And he doesn't want his bosses to know.

"That doesn't happen," he hisses, stepping closer, "unless I prove I've got balls. Unless I prove I can gut a traitor where she stands."

The flat of the knife presses against the gentle swell of my belly.

"I'll make it clean," he whispers. "You'll pay your debt. First I'll cut this bastard out of you. Then, when you watch it suffocate, I'll let you bleed to death."

My whole body locks.

I can't breathe. Can't move.

"Sal—please," I plead, barely able to get the words out.

"You're going to take us to your Russian lover's fancy house. You're going to open the doors, let us in, and then you'll watch him die. You owe me that much."

Tears blur my vision.

The tiny mail room smells like old carpet, cigarettes, and whatever the tenants of the ground floor cook often. The ghosts of my old life taunted me—those first weeks of grief, then trying to settle into a new place. On my own. Even when Sal was there, I always felt alone.

The tip of Sal's knife pierces my sweater, and I flinch. I'm going to die here.

My baby is going to die here.

Unless I do something.

A vibration comes from my pocket, followed quickly by another—Chrissy, probably, texting again. I swallow, keeping my eyes locked on Sal's, and tilt my head slightly.

"You'll never get past his guards," I say.

He laughs. "Oh, I already did, sweety. One of his guys— Lev? Big bastard? We made sure he's out of the picture tonight. Took a few more men than we anticipated, but," Sal shrugs, "he won't be interrupting us tonight."

I gasp.

That blood by the shed.

Lev had been watching the house. Watching *me*.

He'd bled for me.

Sal doesn't wait for me to process. "Let's go."

He waves the blade, and the other two men flank me like bookends of violence.

"I'll scream," I say, voice thin.

"No one's listening," Sal promises with a smirk.

But I knew that's not true.

Not anymore.

Because Konstantin has made sure that someone is *always* listening.

Chapter 24

Konstantin

The message came in as the light dipped behind the skyline.
Coming over.

From Audrey.

My little wolf.

At first glance, the words seem harmless. But something about the cadence sends a cold prickle over the back of my neck. She never just announces her arrival. She asks, or she shows up; there's no in between.

This?

This is rushed. Clipped. Off.

I stand in my office, bathed in the last light of day, and stare at the message. There's another reason I don't trust this.

Only minutes ago, I received a call from the Operator at the Spire. Someone had used the emergency line asking them to contact me and tell me: "She left the house and she's at Magnolia."

That someone was Chrissy, Audrey's best friend and

one of the head accountants. A woman who would definitely *not* be reaching out to me, after recent events, unless something was wrong. The room feels colder than it had a moment before. My thumb hovers over the keys.

Are you alone?

No response.

I type again.

Is Lev bringing you?

Nothing.

I type out another message, this one to Lev, asking where Audrey is—if he's with her.

Again, nothing.

My blood begins to shift, heating, flowing faster. My ribs expand with a breath that comes too tightly. Something is wrong. Deeply, sickeningly wrong.

Lev never fails to check in. He's the best I have, loyal to the bone. Trained like a dog for war.

And he wouldn't leave her. Not unless...

My phone remains dark.

I hit the comm. "Activate perimeter lockdown. No exceptions. Evac protocol one."

The house obeys me.

Steel shutters slide into place with a *hush*. Internal motion detectors ping to life. The townhouse narrows its gaze like a predator in the grass.

Is it overkill? Maybe. Perhaps Audrey just had a long day or is pissed about something that happened at the office, ready to come after me. Maybe she found out that I've insisted she has a six-month maternity leave, fully paid.

Giuseppe's wry smile swims into my memory; his warnings about the blessings and downfalls of having a family. Is having a child making me paranoid before they've even arrived?

I pull my Glock from the drawer beneath the bar, clip it under my jacket, and slide a blade into the sheath hidden in my boot.

Just in time.

The doorbell rings.

Not the side entrance. Not the garage. The *front door*.

Audrey knows, after last time, that she should come in the side. And Lev would never bring her to the front.

I move silently down the hallway, each step a calculation. My hand rests at my side. The gun is ready. I don't need backup, not yet. If this is what I fear, calling for more men would truly be overkill.

Or not enough.

I open the door.

And there she is.

Audrey stands shivering in a pale, thick sweater and house slippers, her buttery leggings hugging her curves. Her hair is half-pinned back; half, because it's fallen. My eyes flicker over her features. Her wide eyes. Her chattering teeth.

"Where's your coat?"

It's a stupid thing to ask, but the instinctive, protective side of me kicks in before the logical side does. Her eyes look up into mine and scream what her lips didn't.

Run.

Stepping to the side, I pull her in with a hand wrapped around her upper arm, her mouth open in a silent shout.

And make the mistake of turning my back.

The first blow slams into the side of my head. Blunt. Hard. Iron. A pipe or a bat. My vision explodes in white.

I go down to one knee, dazed, blinking blood out of my eye. Now Audrey really does scream.

"Konstantin!"

"The study," I grunt, sensing more than seeing forms enter the house behind me. Pain spiders down my jaw and into my ribs as I try to rise. A boot lands in my lower back, but I catch myself as Audrey makes a run for the stairs.

Standing, I spin, gun raised.

Too late.

A second man is already inside. Then a third.

And behind them, closing the door like he belongs here, is Sal Imperi. Even with the dying light behind him, I recognize his lean frame.

The sight of him *in my home* drags rage up from my gut like acid.

"If you touched her—"

One of his men holds up a gun, short and thick, and the action clicks.

Sal smiles like a man who thinks he's still holding the cards.

"Nice place," he says, cocking his head. "Bit sterile, though."

My body surges forward before thought catches up. I can't let them get upstairs, get to *her*. Or the baby.

Desperation, an unfamiliar feeling, makes my skin feel electric. I grab the nearest thug by the throat and slam him into a marble column. Bone cracks. He's thin, wiry, and falls to the ground like nothing. Sal's glance flicks to the body in annoyance.

I fire, but the guy with the gun is surprisingly fast for his size. He manages to duck it and the bullet ricochets somewhere in the foyer. The house, at my earlier command, has become a den of shadows. It's familiar enough to me that I know where to land my feet and brace myself as the bigger thug slams into me, my shoulder buried in his gut.

Sal cracks something heavy over my back. There's a sound of shattering, and I know what it is; an expensive piece of sculpture purchased years ago, a favorite of mine, now in pieces around my feet. I have one hand gripping the thug's, wrapped around his and bending the wrist to point the muzzle of his gun down.

There's a yank and the sound of bullets dropping on the tile.

My gun is gone.

Then a sharp, stinging sensation at my side—familiar. When Sal pulls the knife out, it makes an almost metallic sound. Before he can stick me again I jerk the gun out of his thug's hand, then barrel toward Sal, pinning his right arm and the knife between us.

Audrey screams.

Her scream is what brings me back.

Not the pain.

Not the blood seeping down my hip.

Her.

Because she's here, and she's pregnant. And for the first time in my entire brutal, godless life, I have something to lose.

The future isn't an abstract thing anymore. It's real. It's growing inside her.

Focusing on the bigger man, I drop low, pivot, and drive

my elbow into the bastard's ribs. He gasps. I wrench him forward and crack his skull against my knee.

Sal rushes me then, knife drawn.

But he's underestimated me. I'm not just some slicked-up suit running numbers in a skyscraper. No, what Sal Imperi and the rest of my competition in the city don't know is that I still walk the streets.

I still do my time with the men. On the ground.

I do my dirty work when it needs doing. And *I'm* the Bratva. The monster beneath the bed. The nightmare whispered about in backrooms across three continents.

I catch Sal's wrist mid-swing. Squeeze.

He howls.

The blade drops. I kick it across the floor.

Then Audrey shrieks.

The man whose skull I thought I'd at least fractured is on the stairs, a thick arm wrapped around her throat. Her feet dangle an inch in the air, kicking, her eyes huge in the dark. He hauls her up higher, slamming her sideways into the wall hard enough to make the plaster crack.

Audre makes a broken sound.

The world narrows to a pinpoint.

I shove Sal away. Bend just enough to pull the knife out of my boot, and whip it through the air, praying to a God I don't believe in for the universe to align.

It hits its target, slicing through Audrey's hair just above her ear and plowing through the thug's eye. His arm around her throat loosens, and Audrey crumples as his body folds down the stairs next to her.

Striding forward, I tower over Audrey, listening to the

sickening sound of her labored breath as I pull the blade from the man's eye socket.

When I turn around, Sal Imperi is backing up toward the door.

He points at me, panting. "It didn't have to be like this, Martynov."

"You're right," I say, voice low. "She should have let me kill you months ago."

I jerk my hand back, take aim, and see the glint of the knife as it turns end over end.

It catches Sal in the throat, and he staggers to his knees. In a flash I'm by his side, slowly wrapping my hands around his throat, ignoring the slice of the blade as it bites my finger. I squeeze slowly and steadily until the sound and feel of cracking almost echoes in the atrium. Sal's eyes bulge, blood vessels breaking as he struggles against my hold, legs kicking out wildly.

It takes a long, long time, suffocating someone.

If you aren't careful they'll only pass out.

So, I wait. I tighten my grip.

And Sal Imperi dies in my hands. His pulse slows, then ends against my fingertips.

I turn to Audrey.

She's trying to sit up. Her hands tremble. Blood trickled from her temple, where the knife left a nick, and one hand is pressed to her throat. Her lips are pale.

"Don't move," I say, crouching beside her. "Can you breathe?"

She looks up at me with wide, dazed eyes. Then she whispered something that rips me in half.

"He said he was going to kill the baby."

The rage that follows isn't fire.

It's ice.

"You're bleeding—Konstantin!"

When I turn around, Audrey is trying to stand. I go to her quickly, holding her up and fumbling for my phone with my other hand. Audrey presses her palm to the searing spot just above my hip, the muscle feeling rent and swollen, throbbing. Her hand comes away dark with blood.

"Konstantin—"

"It's okay. I'm calling for help."

Olena picks up and doesn't say anything when I tell her she needs to send men, the Redline, and Ward.

"Wait," I catch myself, looking down at Audrey. "Not Ward. I'm taking Audrey to the hospital. Meet us there."

Audrey tries to take a step and stumbles, still in my arms. I put a hand to her throat, thumb pressed to her windpipe and feel her pulse rocketing.

My voice is gravel when I speak.

"You're safe. I've got you."

Her hand moves to her stomach.

"Is the baby--?"

She nods, faintly. "I think so."

Chapter 25

Audrey

I sink deeper into the stiff VIP hospital mattress, hands resting on my belly, the paper band still around my wrist whispering every time I shift. It's a ridiculous room—high ceilings, filtered light, a built-in espresso machine in the corner, and too many flower arrangements already crowding the table. One bouquet is made entirely of imported peonies, nowhere near possible this time of year. Another has long, drooping calla lilies, probably flown in from some exotic place.

Nana used to say that lilies were for funerals. The memory makes my body clench in anticipation.

It's all absurd.

I'm still shaking.

Everything inside me feels broken and raw. Just hours ago, if I'd made a different decision... if I'd insisted that the landlord forward any packages or double checked my order history. Things might've turned out differently.

Out in the hallway, Konstantin is getting sewn back together while giving orders like it's just another Tuesday. I can hear his voice—low, firm, unrelenting—as he speaks to Olena. Seeing her flash by the window earlier like an angel of death, I no longer felt jealousy.

Now I felt shame.

Guilt.

When her eyes flickered in my direction, I knew she saw me as a threat and a weak spot. Someone who could get —almost *did* get—Konstantin killed.

They're speaking in Russian. I can't understand the words, but I know the tone. It's the sound of war being declared.

It makes my stomach turn.

My hands press down lightly on the swell of my belly. I've been cleared. The doctor said everything looks good, only a little nick that they put bacitracin on from when Sal held the knife to my belly.

The baby is fine. I'm fine. No signs of placental abruption, no internal bleeding, no fractures.

I'm fine.

It doesn't feel like it, though. Taking a deep breath through my nose, I breathe out through my mouth. The nurse in the room glances in my direction with a sweet smile. How much does she know? To her, am I just a rich mother-to-be who's had a scare?

Or does she understand who the man out in the hallway is?

Does *she* know how close I came to getting all three of us murdered tonight? Because I'm sure, without a doubt, that Sal would've followed through on his word after killing Konstantin.

Something inside me cracked the moment the pipe hit

the side of his head. The moment Konstantin shoved me behind him, the moment that thug's knife flashed. I don't think I'll ever be able to unsee it, and the blood pressure machine beeps in warning, the nurse hurrying over to soothe me.

I curl to one side slightly, hugging the pillow. My body remembers the weight of Sal's hand around my throat in the car, the pressure of fear climbing up and choking out everything else. I'd just gotten used to feeling safe again. Letting myself believe I was protected.

But nothing is safe when you belong to Konstantin Martynov.

And that's the problem—I do. Whether I like it or not, I do.

My mind flits to the baby again. *My* baby. I don't know when I started thinking of the pregnancy that way, but it's real now. It feels real. It feels like mine. Not a punishment, not a transaction. A little heartbeat under my ribs. A quiet, vulnerable promise I'm not sure I'll be able to keep.

The doctor steps in with a sigh, murmuring to the nurse, "He's turning down a scan, which is a mistake. Took a nasty hit to the head." He checks my vitals, the baby's vitals, and promises a luxury hospital dinner soon.

My stomach churns at the thought of trying to eat. Outside, the city seems to sink in darkness despite all the lights shining in the buildings.

The door creaks open and Olena appears for just long enough to spear me with a glance sharp enough to draw blood. Her designer coat is folded neatly over one arm, her heels echoing against the tile floor. She doesn't speak—just lets her eyes sweep from my bare feet to the machines behind me. Like she's cataloging everything that makes me unworthy.

Then she disappears.

I can't even muster the energy to be embarrassed. I'm too tired. Too angry at myself.

For getting involved in this.

For stealing the money in the first place.

For falling in love with him.

The door clicks open again. And this time, it's him.

Konstantin enters like a shadow—dressed down now in loose black sweatpants and a bandaged side, no jacket, no tie, just a clean t-shirt stretched tight over blood-stained gauze. There's a dark bruise forming on the side of his head, easy to see as it crawls out of his silver hair. His face looks tired, finally his age, lined with fatigue, pain, and worry.

The man who took a beating for me and didn't even flinch.

There's a smear of blood on his shirt and a wiry man with inked forearms is packing up a stitch kit on the hallway floor.

Konstantin walks straight to the chair beside my bed and sits heavily. No dramatic gestures, no charm.

"Is Olena mad?" It comes out as a whisper. His eyes ghost over my face, then look away—I have my answer.

Ignoring the question, he says, "They're cleaning it now."

"Cleaning what?"

"My townhouse. They're quiet. Efficient. We'll be able to go home soon."

I think of the blood on the marble floor. The shattered

glass. The furniture overturned and the bodies—oh God, the bodies.

Sal is finally gone. *Sal is finally gone.*

I whisper that sentence, scream it, repeat it in my head, but it still doesn't seem real.

"Olena had men sweep the country house." He pauses. "They found Lev."

"He's alive?"

Konstantin's jaw clenches. "Barely. They flew him in. He's in ICU. Surgeon says it will take time... a lot of time. But he's a fighter."

A sob catches in my throat, and I turn my face to the pillow, so he won't see the guilt.

Lev. Always silent. Always there. Protecting me in ways I never asked for. And now he might die because I brought this storm right into Konstantin's house. Into his empire.

What would have happened if, instead of leaving the house, I'd locked the door? Called Kashmere from upstairs and texted Konstantin about the blood, the scuff marks?

Why was I so stupid to think that violence couldn't reach me there?

Because he promised you, a small voice comments in the back of my head. It's accusatory, bitter, and it takes the edge off of my guilt—but only a little.

"I'm sorry," I whisper.

Konstantin shifts slightly, glancing at me with a look I can't decipher. The swelling in his face has gone down, but his expression is pale steel.

"I'm sorry you had to see that."

I shake my head quickly, not wanting both of us to

waste time or emotions on regret. "You had to, Konstantin. If you hadn't he would have..."

"He would have killed you. And the child." His voice is measured, cold. Stating a fact. It chills me to the bone, how matter-of-fact he is about this. "That's not a line you cross and live."

"Why... why didn't they just...? At the country house?"

I can't seem to put the words together. A pounding headache is creeping in at my temples and suddenly, I'm exhausted. A nurse opens the door, slips in, and sets down a tray of grilled chicken with vegetables. The smell churns my stomach.

Konstantin understands what I'm asking, and his answer makes it clear that he's all business. *This* is what it's like being on the receiving end of Konstantin Martynov's cold brilliance.

"I was the end goal, not you. He still needed you to get to me Audrey. But if something had gone wrong, if Lev had been there to back me up..."

Then the words spill out, quiet and broken: "I don't think I can do this anymore."

The events of the last few hours flash before my eyes.

The blood. The pounding of my pulse in my ears. Feeling the baby shift; the fear of not feeling the baby at all.

And Konstantin, on his knees, eyes unfocused.

He doesn't move.

His eyes go distant. Something closes behind them, like a vault. When he speaks again, it's with the flat voice of a man who's already started dying.

"I see."

I shake my head, fighting back tears. "That's not—it's not that I don't want to—I just—"

"You're scared." He's still staring at the wall. "You should be."

"I'm not scared of you." I pause. "Not like that."

"Then what are you scared of Audrey?"

I sit up slowly, brushing a hand through my tangled hair. I can feel the tears now, balancing in my lashes, stubborn and hot.

"I'm scared that I'm not going to survive this. That I'll never be anything more than bait. A weapon someone else uses against you. That someday you'll get shot and not get back up. That someday our child will watch me die because someone wants to hurt you. I'm scared of losing you."

That makes him look at me.

His voice is a whisper now. "You think I don't lie awake every night afraid of the same things?"

I bite my lip, hands tingling with anxiety.

"I didn't plan this," he continues. "Didn't plan to want you. To need you. But I do. You're the only thing I can't control. And that terrifies me."

My heart stutters painfully, and I try to hold onto the resolve I walked in with. When Konstantin carried me out to the waiting car I knew. When my hand slipped in his blood in the back seat, *I knew.* So why is this so hard?

I try to remember that I was going to end this. That I was going to walk away.

But I can't.

Because now I see him clearly.

Konstantin Martynov—the man who built an empire out of blood and ash—is broken in front of me. Human.

I'd be lying to myself if I said I didn't realize I was in love with him until this moment. No, I've known for a while now. It's impossible not to love this man with the way he loses himself in me, and the way he makes me feel alive again.

But I *have* been lying to myself. Telling myself he can keep me safe.

That everything will turn out fine.

That maybe I can stay, and make this work... me, Konstantin, our baby.

He saved me, and he's powerful, but he doesn't know how to love softly. Because even when he's trying not to feel, he feels everything too deeply.

He wouldn't *have* to save me if I was never in danger to begin with. And that's why I have to end this.

I can see the way he looks at me, the way he clings to control because if he lets go, he'll drown in it. I will be his downfall if I stay.

He'll burn the world to keep me. And it'll destroy him.

So, I gather the strength I don't have and say the words that taste like blood.

"I'm going to leave."

He stiffens.

"Not yet," I say quickly. "Not today. But... after the baby's born. After everything's safe. I need to go, like we planned..."

When had that plan changed? When did we *both* start assuming I would stay?

I can see in his face, the way it breaks, that he thought we could make it work. He doesn't speak or look at me, and it makes my heart cave in.

"I'll go to the west coast. I think I... I think I should take the baby with me, Konstantin. They'll be safe with me." *And not with you.* The words go unspoken, but he flinches, and I rush on: "And you'll be able to breathe again. You won't have to look over your shoulder every time someone gets too close to me. You won't be *vulnerable*."

His fingers clench on his knee.

The silence between us is deafening. It's not rejection. It's surrender.

And that's almost worse.

A small part of me wanted him to fight, to argue. To demand that I stay.

But he won't, because he knows I'm right.

"I'll make sure you have everything you need," he says at last, voice strangled. "Protection. A place. Money. Anything."

"I don't want anything."

"Then you'll get it anyway."

He stands.

The movement is slow, painful. Blood seeps through the edge of the gauze again. But he doesn't react to the pain he must be feeling. He just moves toward the door, like something in him has turned off.

"Konstantin—" I start, reaching for him.

He doesn't turn. The door clicks behind him, and I know that he won't come back.

I'll give you everything. That's what he said to me, once —and Konstantin Martynov doesn't break promises.

Chapter 26

Konstantin

The penthouse smells new. Not fresh—*new*. Cold concrete, virgin lacquer, brushed steel fixtures and faint ozone from recently installed wiring. A property that's never been lived in, touched only by designers and cleaners.

I don't like it.

Still, it's necessary. The townhouse is compromised—riddled with ghosts. My blood dried into the marble. Audrey's scent still in the air, clinging to the high-thread-count sheets I burned the same day I was released from the hospital.

I gave the order to sell it that afternoon. Had it wrapped up through my own real estate firm to keep it quiet. Transferred to shell ownership in two hours flat. All of it arranged through Satin.

They're already waiting when I arrive.

Leaning against the far wall of the elevator lobby, all tailored steel-gray slacks and an asymmetric turtleneck, Satin is a modern sculpture come to life. They wear their long black hair in a single braid down the center of their back, geometric silver jewelry catching the mid-morning light.

Their expression is, as always, unreadable.

"Mr. Martynov," they purr, offering the keys between two perfectly polished fingers. "Welcome home."

I take the keys. They're cold.

"This place was just finished last month. Custom design. Over seven thousand square feet. Black walnut, brushed steel, radiant floors, smart glass on every window. You'll love the view."

I step past them into the main room.

The view is fine.

Manhattan stretches beyond the floor-to-ceiling windows, a glittering river of ambition and rot. I stare out at it and feel... nothing.

Behind me, Satin's heels click once on the slate tile. "You want a walkthrough?"

"No."

"Understood."

There's a pause. I hear it before I see it—the calculation in their voice, the curiosity that no one else would dare express.

"I've heard a rumor," they say lightly. "That congratulations are in order."

I turn slowly.

Satin is smiling with their mouth, not their eyes. Their fingers worry the end of the braid; the only sign they're anxious, wondering if they're overstepping.

"Is it true?" they ask. "A child?"

The word hits harder than expected.

Child.

I say nothing, which is answer enough.

Satin's gaze flickers, and the smile fades. "Be careful, Konstantin. In this city, rumors spread like blood in water. And children... children make people stupid."

My eyes narrow.

They back off, gracefully.

"Enjoy the property," they murmur, already heading for the private elevator. "It's a fortress, but even fortresses fall. Ask Troy."

The doors close behind them with a whisper.

Silence reclaims the space.

I walk the penthouse alone. It's beautiful, in that soulless way—which feels like fate. A soulless man in a soulless place. Dark wood panels glow under downlights, everything sleek and masculine. The furniture is all angles and sharp lines, untouched. The kitchen is chef-grade.

I shake off memories of Audrey in an apron, flour powdered against her jaw. Her wide eyes the night she told me. *I'm pregnant.*

The bedroom is cavernous. I practically run there, away from the apparition, but it doesn't do me any good. We found so many places to fuck, so many to make love, not all of them beds—but I doubt I'll ever be able to sleep again.

The townhouse wasn't *home* before Audrey stepped inside. It was a place I went back to every night, a place I liked the look of. The rooms wrapped around me, and it felt safe, largely in part due to the security system and the years I spent there.

This place... this place doesn't know me yet.

I pause at the kitchen island, laying the keys down flat.

My hand lingers over them, fingers tracing the steel edge.

Audrey's face flickers into my mind. The way she looked in that hospital bed. Pale. Shaken. Defiant.

The way she whispered that she didn't think she could do this anymore. That being with me—being near me—was going to get her and the baby killed.

She's right.

I am not a safe man, never have been, and never will be. I've come too far, to the very edge of the world—possibly over it and into hell.

At least that's what it feels like now.

To have a taste of what could be and lose it. This must be how Adam and Eve felt, pushed out of Eden, tart apple still on their tongues. Knowing too much: what they could have had.

What they lost.

No matter how much I want to protect her, no matter what I feel when I watch her laugh, or cry, or press her palm to her stomach like she's already cradling the child—our child.

A boy, maybe. Or a girl. I don't care, but my chest aches with the fact that I'll never know.

Could I hunt them down? Follow Audrey to the ends of the earth, pay someone to watch her, to divulge her medical records? Yes, but will I?

What matters is that they'll grow up with a target on their back. Because they're mine.

The only way I can give them a good life is to never look for them again.

I sink into the nearest chair.

I should give her up. Let her go. Let her take the baby. Send them as far from New York as they can go. Disappear them in the Arctic Circle if I have to. It would feel good to walk across an endless, cold landscape and let the frost steal my breath. In Russia it was talked of often; people who, drunk, wandered out into the winter wasteland. Fell asleep. Slipped away.

I look at her and I don't just see beauty or lust—I see salvation. I see the version of myself I could've been, if the world hadn't taught me to sharpen my soul into a blade. Maybe I would have done things differently all those decades ago if I had known *she* would be waiting for me here in New York.

But Audrey is right--loving her is a weakness. Wanting this child is a weakness.

Olena said as much, has been forceful of it, sure that I'll lose Martynov Global Holdings. That just one loose tooth in this system I've created could take me out if they sense weakness.

That's not even taking into consideration men like Giuseppe, or my other enemies. I've made plenty of them over the years.

Olena arrives hours later, uninvited, and lets herself in. I don't bother asking how she got a key, though I wonder if Satin and she talked about their misgivings.

The penthouse door clicks softly, and she steps inside in a black trench coat, head freshly shaved and gleaming like a knife.

She surveys the space with a critical eye.

"You've upgraded."

"Did I?"

She takes a slow turn, then fixes me with that sharp gaze. "You needed an untainted place."

I say nothing, tamping down the rage that threatens to burst my veins. This isn't time to turn against my own. Olena has been by my side for years; I trust her with my life. And *she* isn't the one who made a mistake.

I am.

She walks toward me, heels muffled on the expensive tile. She stops three feet away.

"I assume Satin filled you in."

"I didn't ask for gossip."

"You should. Because everyone's talking, Konstantin."

Her arms cross over her chest.

"You're distracted."

I raise a brow. "I'm recovering."

"You've been recovered for days. You haven't attended a single meeting. Haven't reviewed the expansion in Macau. The weapons shipment in Tunis. You're barely holding the board's attention, and they're starting to look for other sources of power. By the way, the auction house in Upstate New York is doing well. Not that you asked."

I lean back.

Olena has always known how to strike where it hurts.

"You're worried," she says. "About her. The child. The future."

It's not a question. I meet her gaze. "You ever wonder what we're building, Olena?"

Her mouth twists. "Power. Legacy."

"And what's the point of a legacy if I'm dead before I can give it to anyone?"

Her eyes soften, just a fraction. Like me, Olena escaped a past that didn't want her. But I've never asked her: what does *she* want? What does she long for?

And is it not another person, a companion? A legacy?

"You think this child will save you?"

"No," I whisper. "I think I'll destroy them."

She sighs, stepping closer. "Then let them go."

"I can't."

"Then make them strong." Her words land like a slap.

I watch her cross the room, pour herself a drink from the bar, and perch on the edge of a low-slung leather chair. Probably the first person to ever set her skinny Russian ass on it.

"You lost Mikhail," she says softly.

I flinch.

That name is never spoken.

My younger brother. Caught in a street war that wasn't his, all because a gang back home wanted to make an example of me. *Think you can leave here, succeed, without us?* I'd been running money, a mule, for them for a while. Until I left.

The *poitsiya* found him.

"He was your first weakness," Olena says. "This one—

Audrey, the child—they're your second. The difference is you let Mikhail go. You have to let them go, too, Konstantin."

Did I ever let Mikhail go?

I stare down at my hands. Calloused. Steady. The hands that built this empire.

The hands that bled to keep it.

Olena sets the drink down without taking a sip. "Fix it, Konstantin. Or lose everything."

Night falls. The penthouse doesn't feel any more or less empty.

I pace the long hallway between the kitchen and the windows, glass in hand, drinking something older than most of the men I've killed. I should sleep, but it's been impossible, as if the fight is still happening—as if I'm still on my knees in the atrium, the thug at my back, the pipe's metallic *clang*.

Outside, the city pulses.

Inside, the cut at my waist throbs. I could make one call and get painkillers to dull it, but vodka does the same just fine.

At two-fifteen in the morning, my phone rings.

Not the secure line—the personal line.

For a moment I hope it's her. Audrey changing her mind. Asking me to come back. I haven't made her leave the country house, can't bring myself to do it, but Kashmere has reached out to say she's been packing. Slowly. Agonizingly.

As if she's considering...

225

But the name that flashes onto the screen is that of my enemy. Sartorre. It shouldn't surprise me. I did, after all, kill three of his men only a few nights ago.

I answer without speaking.

He chuckles.

"You're up."

"You always call this late?"

"Only when I know you're not sleeping." There's still an edge of an accent to his words, though he, like me, tried hard to assimilate.

I pace to the window. "What do you want?"

"I heard about Sal," he says casually. "Can't say I'll miss him. Thank you."

"You confirmed it, then. That he was leading the coup."

"I suspected. In the last days, he went rogue. Stopped answering my calls. Made demands he didn't earn. You did me a favor, Konstantin."

I grit my teeth.

Giuseppe's voice is smoother than the wine he traffics. "You've made a mess, but not one you can't clean. I trust Redline's already been."

I say nothing.

He hums. "And how is your family?"

The silence stretches.

"I'm not going to threaten you," he adds. "That's not what this is."

"Then what is it?"

"A warning."

"Go on."

He exhales. "When I was younger, I thought having a family would be a liability. I kept everything separate. Wife

226

in the countryside, kids in boarding school. I thought I was protecting them."

"And?"

"They grew up strangers. Afraid of me. Of my name. My business. That's why Rocco is such an ass. But Fia, we pulled her out of school, had her taught in private. After... well, you don't need to hear about that. There are some things you can't protect your children from Konstantin. The point is, Fia was the only one around to see my work. I was scared when she was with me, yes, but I'd seen what the world would do to them even if I wasn't there. So, I brought the boys home. There's still a rift... a chasm we can't seem to span..."

I let that hang in the air.

He chuckles bitterly. "You have a chance to do something different. Don't waste it."

"Why are you telling me this?"

"Because I know what it's like to live in a penthouse full of ghosts."

The line goes dead.

I stand in the dark long after the call ends.

The vodka bottle is half-empty. My soul feels the same.

I want to call Audrey. I want to beg her to come here, to see this place. To sit in that chair, to lie in that bed, to let me worship her swollen belly and promise I'll be better. Safer. Smarter. That I'll walk away from it all.

But I can't promise that.

I'm a man soaked in blood. Anything I touch will eventually drown.

I walk to the bedroom, strip down, and climb into a bed that still smells like packaging plastic and bleach. Sleep doesn't come, and I don't expect it to.

Instead, with my eyes closed, all I can picture is Audrey in a dress soft as sunlight. Holding our child against her chest.

And me—watching from the outside.

I don't know if I'm strong enough to stay away.

But I know I have to try, for them. For once in my goddamn life—something other than vengeance.

Chapter 27

Audrey

I t's been six weeks since the night everything changed. Six weeks since Sal's body was found in a shipping container off the Brooklyn docks, his face almost unrecognizable. No suspects, no witnesses or leads. The cops didn't bother tracking me down; I was just an ex-girlfriend.

Or maybe Martynov Global Holdings requested a favor. Maybe there's no question, for the NYPD, who did it, and they know pursuit is pointless.

It's been six weeks since I saw Konstantin Martynov. Since I felt his hands on my waist, his voice in my ear, the heat of his gaze burning through me like truth.

I rest my palm against the swell of my belly as I lie on the couch, staring at the ceiling of my new apartment. It's nice—bigger than the one on Magnolia, newly renovated, and quiet. There's a washer-dryer in the unit and a doorman downstairs who always offers to carry my groceries. A second-floor walk-up would've been cheaper, but the salary Konstantin left me with before he disappeared makes it hard to justify anything less. Plus, I can't imagine a walk-up when my feet and lower back hurt as much as they do.

Guilt makes me shift uncomfortably on the couch. The apartment is comfortable, better than anything I could've asked for... and I *didn't* ask for it. For the money that purchased it.

The money that feels like hush money.

A job came quickly after that—a remote contract role for a private medical office upstate. I review their books, clean up their billing, and make sure no one's double-charging for root canals. It's work I can do in my sleep.

And sometimes, I do, because I'm exhausted. It's hard to tell if the exhaustion is physical or mental or both. Both would make sense; it feels like I've tripled in size the last few weeks, and every single time I see Chrissy she exclaims, "How are you even *bigger!?*" Some days it's hard not to take that as an insult, but most days I'm just happy that baby and I are safe and healthy.

This is the life I thought I wanted—safe, quiet, clean. No blood smears, no threats, no staying up at night wondering if he's okay.

And yet, I'm lonelier than I've ever been.

Konstantin hasn't called. Not once. Not even a text. There was only a message, hand-delivered three days after we were released from the hospital. One of his men showed up on my doorstep, tall, scarred, and soft-spoken, holding a single white envelope.

The note inside was simple and direct. *No one will ever touch you again.*

My fingers itch with the desire to go get it, where I

tucked it away in my nightstand. I've read it so often that the thick cardstock is already worn at the fold-over.

Aside from that note, I haven't heard from Konstantin at all. Pregnancy hormones have me swinging wildly back and forth between *Doesn't he care about us at all?* and *Fuck him! I don't need him!* **We** *don't need him!*

And that's true, but... I miss him so much it makes my throat ache.

Realistically, I can't be upset with him. This is exactly what I asked for—to be safe.

The baby shifts under my hand and I exhale slowly, sitting up. My back cracks from the hours spent curled into this couch like a shell. I pull on a hoodie, tug my hair into a loose braid, and decide to walk to the library.

Maybe if I'm surrounded by books, I'll remember what it's like to be someone else for a little while.

The library is half-full, the way it always is in early afternoon—students dozing over textbooks, retirees flipping through cookbooks, the occasional couple tucked into the fiction section like they're starring in their own meet-cute.

I drift toward the familiar stacks, trailing my fingers over the shelves without reading the spines. It's more muscle memory than anything. You'd think with so much time now, working remote and not feeling up to going out, I'd be able to read. But my brain feels fuzzy and unfocused most days, on top of the exhaustion.

Emil appears from between two shelves, the small re-shelving cart behind him.

"Audrey!" His blue eyes, crinkled at the corners, scan me quickly. "It's been a few weeks, darling. How are you? How's the baby?"

"Good," I answer with a tired smile, automatically resting a hand on top of my belly.

"You're glowing," he insists, making me laugh. He says it every time I've seen him, and I try to make it to the library once a week. That first week—only days out of the hospital —was nerve-wracking. I wasn't sure how Emil would feel about my situation... not that I explained *who* the baby daddy was, but it was embarrassing enough that he wasn't in my life.

Emil took it all in stride. I shouldn't have worried so much. He'd only hugged me, tears in his eyes, and whispered, "Raena would be so happy."

Then we were *both* in tears, because thinking of my Nana did that a lot—especially when I felt so unmoored without her, so unsure of whether or not she'd approve.

Emil pulls me into a one-armed hug, gentle and fast, stepping back quickly when he realizes how much larger I've gotten since the last time he saw me.

He studies me with warm eyes. "Your Nana would be so thrilled. I mean that. You know how much she loved babies. She used to knit those tiny socks for strangers."

"I still have three pairs." They'd been in her dresser, the last set half-finished.

He laughs. "Of course you do. God, she'd be so proud of you. Doing this on your own. Brave girl."

Something twists in my chest.

"How are you? I'll be on lunch soon—do you want to step out, get something at the little food truck on the

232

corner?" His enthusiasm is infectious, and I know I can at least look forward to the baby having a grandfather figure in his future.

"No, thank you though. I'm just trying to get out of the house today; I'm pretty beat." The exhaustion is catching up to me again. If I sit down in any of the armchairs scattered across the library, I'll probably pass out for hours. "I'm happy I got to see you though. Would you like to come over for dinner soon?"

He nods, and we plan for a day and time. Just before I turn around, Emil says my name again, reaching into his pocket and pulling out a folded note. "I saw a poem yesterday that made me think of you. It's short."

I take it, try not to tear up. "Thanks, Emil."

"Be careful, Audrey. Call me if you need anything."

The offer makes me feel just a *little* less alone.

* * *

The apartment is too quiet when I get home.

The couch still holds the imprint of where I sat this morning. The kitchen smells like tea and toast. I set Emil's poem on the counter, telling myself I'll read it later. Maybe.

There's a knock at the door just before five. I startle. For a moment, my heart kicks like it's him. Like he's finally here. Then it plummets in fear. PTSD will do that to you. Even with Sal dead, it still feels like someone's out to get me.

But it's only Chrissy, juggling takeout and a grocery bag.

"Hey, I brought soup and ice cream," she says, brushing

past me into the kitchen. "Also, you need more bread. And whatever weird pregnancy juice you keep drinking."

"Coconut water."

"That."

She dumps everything onto the counter, tosses her coat over the back of a chair, and fixes me with a look. "You haven't been answering your texts."

"Sorry, my stomach has been off. And I've been tired."

"Hence the soup," she brandishes the container, raising her brows. "You've been hiding."

I sigh. "Don't start."

"I'm not starting anything. I'm just..." She pauses, pouring the soup into a bowl. "I'm worried about you."

"I'm fine."

"You're miserable."

I sit slowly. The baby gives a little kick, as if to agree with her.

Chrissy leans her elbows on the counter. "When was the last time you talked to him?"

"I haven't."

She blinks. "What do you mean?"

"I mean... he hasn't called. I haven't seen him since the hospital. Since that night." My voice cracks, and I look away. "He sent a message. That was it."

Chrissy stares at me. "You're telling me you're carrying this man's baby, and he hasn't even checked in?"

Okay, so maybe I hadn't told Chrissy everything... "Chris, I... I told him I didn't want to do this anymore."

She snorts. "It's a little late for that."

"*With him,*" I clarify, rolling my eyes.

She's quiet for a long moment. "You told Konstantin

Martynov, the man who you basically had a contract with to fuck you pregnant, that you didn't want to raise a baby with him?"

God, it sounds bad when she says it like that. "...Yes."

"And you didn't feel like that was an important thing to explain. This whole time I thought he'd just dumped you, Audrey, and the baby."

Shame tears through me like a fire, feeding the nausea. I push the bowl of soup away. "I know, I know, it's just... it was easier to let Konstantin be the villain."

"Mmm. A man like him, it usually is, right?" Chrissy's eyes are sharp, a reprimand. Letting her, or anyone, think that he's some loser who walks away from his child was wrong. Especially when I literally asked for it.

"I'm sorry. I should've told you everything." Taking a deep breath, I explain that night in the hospital. "I just couldn't see a way forward then. A way for me and the baby, or Konstantin, to be safe."

She softens. "Audrey... I've never seen you like this. You loved him."

I nod.

"And he loved you."

I look down.

"He still does," she adds. "Men like that... they don't know how to let go. He's only keeping his distance because you told him to, which proves just how much he's obsessed with you. Because you told him it was the only option."

Tears sting my eyes. "What if it is?"

"Then that's your decision. But if it's not—if what you want is to fight for this—then fight for it."

I shake my head. "I don't know where he is."

"Then find him."

There's a problem, though—a man like Konstantin Martynov could find anyone. He has the resources, the manpower, the resolve.

I'm just a woman in love.

* * *

It's almost dark when the cab pulls up outside the townhouse. "Can you wait?" I ask the driver, who glances in the mirror before nodding. He doesn't seem to recognize, or care, where we are. Which is a good thing.

Stepping out of the car, I tilt my head back and look up. The windows are black. The driveway is empty. The house looks like it's sleeping.

I step up to the front door and knock.

Nothing.

No guards materializing out of the darkness, no security system clicking and humming to life. I try the buzzer anyway. Wait. Knock again.

Still nothing.

He's gone.

I'm halfway back down the steps when a familiar voice murmurs behind me.

"You're persistent."

I spin, nearly losing my balance despite being in flats.

Olena stands on the sidewalk, dressed in slate gray, a cigarette between her fingers and a look of thinly veiled amusement on her face.

"How long have you been watching me?" I ask, catching my breath.

"Long enough to see you pout like a petulant child." Then her features twist from amusement to something sour. "Longer. A few weeks now."

That information sinks in. I'm tempted to ask if that was Konstantin's idea—or hers. But Olena isn't the kind of woman to chat, to give all her secrets away, so I ask the most important question instead: "Do you know where he is?"

She smirks. "You're not very subtle."

"I'm not trying to be."

Olena's eyes drift to my belly, then back to my face. "You look healthy."

"Thanks."

"And foolish."

"Also, thanks."

She takes a long drag on the cigarette, then flicks the ash to the side. "He's not here."

"I gathered."

"He doesn't want to be found."

"I don't care."

That catches her off guard. Just for a second. She does a double-take. "You're ballsy," she says finally. "I'll give you that."

"Where is he, Olena?"

"Even if I wanted to tell you, I couldn't."

"Why?"

"Because he made me swear I wouldn't."

I deflate, shoulders sagging, and fight the pressure building between my eyes. Crying on the street, in front of a woman who is basically an assassin, and doesn't want me anywhere near her boss, would not be a good move.

"So, he's really done with me then." The cab's brake

237

lights go off, and the car inches forward a bit. The driver has finally noticed me talking to a tall, impassive, bald woman standing in the shadows. *Now* he's nervous. I move to turn away, then pause. "Can you just tell me if he's okay?"

Olena looks at me for a long time.

"No," she says quietly. "But he's alive. And he's trying."

I nod, swallowing the lump in my throat. Behind her, the streetlight flickers on.

"I just need to talk to him," I whisper. "Please."

She takes one last drag, then crushes the cigarette beneath her heel.

"If he wants to find you," she says, turning away, "he will."

Then she disappears into the dark.

And I'm left standing on the steps of an empty house, more certain than ever of one thing—I'm not done fighting.

Chapter 28

Konstantin

When the call comes I'm in the study, blinds drawn against the night, watching the soft flicker of security footage on the corner monitor. Audrey's apartment has been quiet for hours. Lev's men confirm she hasn't left. Her building is locked down tighter than a vault.

It's after midnight and my private line buzzes. The name flashing on the screen surprises me; we haven't spoken since I took down the coup meant to take him out.

"*Da.*"

"Konstantin," Giuseppe's smooth voice slithers down the line, lightly accented. With the last few months behind us, the emotions that surface catch me off guard; for the first time ever his voice sparks a sense of calm in me. Sartorre has become, oddly, a kind of father-figure. Not that that would stop him from killing me someday. "I thought you might want to know... your girl just walked into my front door."

For a second, I don't speak.

The world tilts.

"My girl?" I ask carefully, though I already know the answer.

"Audrey Wolfe. Small, dark hair, big eyes, soft mouth. She asked for you like she owned the place. Ballsy thing. I have to admit, I admire it."

I'm already moving. Pulling on my jacket. Texting Lev to have the driver pull up and have his gun loaded and ready. The click of my own holster is louder than it should be in the silence.

"What does she want?"

"To find you," Giuseppe replies lazily. "Says no one will tell her where you've been. And considering how hot she looked when she stormed in? Can't blame her for getting desperate. Hell, if I was a younger man—"

Some things never change.

"If you touch her, I'll paint your walls with your blood."

There's a pause. Then a low chuckle. "I apologize, Konstantin. I just meant to comment on her beauty. And ferocity. She's fine, in one piece. The boys know to leave her alone. I'm calling because, despite our truce, you're not the only one with enemies. You should know where your queen is moving on the board."

The line goes dead.

Lev is already in the foyer, his eyes and gun glinting in the dark.

"Car. Now."

We don't speak on the way. Lev knows better. His silence is a weapon sharper than any blade, but I can feel his tension crackling beside me. He's the best soldier I have, but that doesn't change the fact that only weeks ago he was released to get back to his "normal" life. Of course, the doctors didn't know what he gets up to in his spare time; running down men almost as bad as him, slitting throats. He's good at what he does, and I'm sure part of the tension in his shoulders comes from *almost* being killed.

He knows this could be a setup. That Giuseppe might be luring me in, tired of playing nice.

I don't care.

I'd walk into a death trap blindfolded if Audrey was inside it.

She came looking for me.

It shouldn't undo me the way it does, but it does.

She came to them—walked into the lion's den—because I disappeared. Because I made myself scarce, convinced myself that was what she wanted. That she'd be better off.

Has she really changed her mind?

Hope rises in my chest, unfamiliar and warm.

When we pull up outside the Sartorre compound, Lev's eyes flick to me. I nod once, and he steps out first. Two guards flank the door—posturing, expensive suits, hands near their guns. They don't move.

"Tell Giuseppe I'm here," I growl.

One disappears. The other just looks at me like I'm already dead.

I wait.

Fifteen seconds.

Twenty.

The lock clicks.

They let us in.

I walk through the gilded doors of Giuseppe's headquarters like I own the place, because fear is a luxury I stopped affording decades ago. The floors are marble, the air tinged with cologne, money, and blood. Lev shadows me like death itself.

Down the corridor, past flickering sconces, and lingering eyes. Sartorre's place is never empty. His guests, the worst of the worst men and women in the world, rotate through luxurious rooms, fed anything they desire.

Then—

There.

Audrey.

She's sitting in a velvet chair in the gallery, spine straight, arms crossed tightly over her chest like armor. Her eyes snap to mine the moment I enter.

Her mouth parts. She stands.

And the only thing I can think is *Thank God*.

I cross the space without blinking, without a single word for Giuseppe or the men watching from the balconies above. I don't care about the statement this makes—about how unhinged it looks for Konstantin Martynov to crash into enemy territory over a woman.

Let them whisper. Let them wonder.

Let them know she matters.

"Audrey." My voice is too low, too rough. Moving through the room is like moving through a maze, or a massive chess board, sculptures and statues littering the checked floor. I reach her in three long strides.

She's trembling, but her eyes are fierce. Already she's so much bigger than she was in the hospital—but it's gorgeous on her, the way she carries it at her hips, her shoulders back and full breasts pushed out.

"No one would tell me where you were."

"You shouldn't have come here."

"What was I supposed to do? I left messages. I went to the Spire. Olena said you were busy and—"

"I was protecting you."

"I don't need protection. I need answers. I need *you*."

Silence surges between us, thick and sharp as a blade.

Her lips tremble before she swallows hard and wipes at her cheek. Furious at the tears. "You just disappeared."

"I know. I thought that's what you wanted."

She draws a deep breath in. "I did too, at first, but..."

"I thought you were done with me."

"I'm never done with you."

I can't take it anymore. I grab her hand, pull her against me. Her body crashes into mine, and I feel it—the heat, the rage, the relief. She struggles for half a second, then folds against my chest, our child between us.

I hold her like I've just ripped her back from the brink of death. That's what it feels like, Eurydice and Orpheus but in reverse. I was walking straight into hell, a ghost, and Audrey came after me.

Giuseppe appears in the archway, drink in hand, watching like it's a show.

I meet his eyes and give him the coldest nod of my life, a small smile on his lips.

Then I walk out, with Audrey's hand in mine.

Let the whole fucking city see.

I'll never let her go.

The car is silent. She won't look at me.

Tears dry on her cheeks, but her arms are crossed, body

tucked into the far corner of the leather seat. It kills me, the distance. Lev rides up front, the privacy glass up and fogged.

"You going to yell at me now?" she asks tightly. "Because I really don't feel like being punished for this. I did what I had to."

I don't answer. I've been trying to find the words since the moment we left Giuseppe's compound, but they just won't come.

How can I beg for forgiveness, thank her, promise her everything, chastise her, all at once? Everything I want to say tangles and sits heavy in my throat.

"Olena said you wouldn't see me," she whispers, staring out the window. "She said you were too busy. Didn't want me to know where you were and would kill her if she told me."

"She's right," I answer gruffly. Hurt flashes across Audrey's face, and she tucks into herself somehow even more.

"I have been busy. She told me you came looking. But I had things to do. I buried Sal, burned his contacts. Hunted down the mole in the Spire and made an example of them. Your friend is safe," I assure her at her startled gasp. "In fact, she's the one who led me to them. I needed time, Audrey, after what you said to me."

I reach into my coat pocket.

Pull out the small black box I've been carrying for weeks.

When I open it, the diamond catches the light between us.

Audrey stares. Her gorgeous eyes catch on mine.

"You think I disappeared because I was done with you?" My voice is low, lethal. "You think I stayed away because I wanted to?"

Her eyes are wide, a hand resting on top of her belly.

She swallows.

"I'm obsessed with you, Audrey Wolfe. From the moment I saw you. From the first damn time you told me no." I reach across the seat, sliding the ring onto her trembling hand. "You are mine. And now you're going to be my wife."

She covers her mouth. Her eyes brim.

And for the first time since I met her, she's speechless.

"I love you," I say, the only truth I've ever known. "You're my obsession. My salvation. My punishment. I don't care what anyone thinks. I don't care if it makes me look weak. I'd burn this city to the ground for you."

Then she's in my arms.

Then she's kissing me like she's drowning and I'm the only breath she has left.

* * *

The Spire is dark when we arrive.

Lev disappears like smoke. The elevators are empty, the floor silent.

I barely get her into my office before I have her pressed against the wall, her dress hiked up, her legs around my waist. Her fingers tangle in my hair. My mouth crushes against hers like I'm starving.

"I'm going to marry you," I growl against her neck, biting just hard enough to make her gasp. "You're going to carry my name and my child. And everyone who ever looked at you sideways is going to *fear* you."

"Yes," she breathes, gasping as I tear her panties. "Yes, Konstantin—"

I slam her onto the desk. Sweep the files off with one hand.

Her legs fall open. Just the scent of her, burned into my brain, is enough to make me hard. I press my palm to her slick heat, groaning at how ready she is.

"You came for me," I rasp. "You came *through them* for me."

"I had to," she whispers. "I love you."

My control snaps.

I slam into her with a growl, one hand gripping her thigh, the other tangled in her hair as I thrust hard, deep, claiming her. Her cries echo off the walls, desperate, hungry, pleading.

She's mine.

She's *always* been mine.

And now the world will know it.

Chapter 29

Audrey

I t happens in the early hours of the morning. A slow, curling pressure wakes me—not pain exactly, just something deeper than discomfort. Like my body is a bell being rung gently from within. I sit up slowly, holding my breath, and wait for it to pass.

Konstantin sleeps like the dead next to me, his large body stretched across the bed. The blackout curtains paint the bedroom black, but I sense him there—my protector.

The pain passes, eventually. A slow tide easing back.

I glance at the clock.

3:14 a.m.

The penthouse is dark, quiet except for the faint hum of the security system and the soft rhythm of Konstantin's breathing beside me. I'm too awake to sleep now, alert for—what? Standing, I walk to the windows and gently shift one of the heavy shades. The city glitters far below, a frozen sea of golds and silvers stretching to the horizon.

Another wave rolls through me. This one a little firmer. A little sharper.

I inhale. Exhale.

Okay.

I think... this is it.

And weirdly, I'm not panicking. Not even a little. Maybe it's the hours of breathing techniques I practiced. Or the fact that I packed the hospital bag two weeks ago and triple-checked it last night. Or maybe it's just that the man sleeping beside me has made me feel safer in the last three months than I've ever felt in my entire life.

I reach out and place a hand on his bare shoulder.

"Konstantin," I whisper.

He doesn't stir.

I lean in closer, pressing a kiss to the space behind his ear. "Konstantin. Wake up."

His body tenses immediately—habit. That instinct to protect hardwired into every nerve. His eyes open. Alert. Dangerous.

Then they soften the moment they meet mine.

"What's wrong?"

I smile gently. "It's time."

His expression doesn't change at first. Then he blinks.

"Time for what?"

I wait.

His eyes widen slowly as the words register.

"You mean—"

"Yes."

He sits up, completely awake now. "You're in labor."

"I can't imagine what else this would be." Another wave of pain rolls through me, slowly, hunching my body over. I brace both hands on the bed, breathing deeply. Konstantin watches, eyes wide and poised to do... what? The look of helplessness on his face makes me laugh breathlessly.

"Oh f—okay. Okay. Stay there."

He bolts out of bed like it's a hostage situation. Which, to be fair, might be the only other thing that would jolt him into this level of motion before dawn. I can't help grinning as I watch him stumble into a pair of black pants, then hesitate like he's trying to remember what clothes are.

"Konstantin," I say gently, "I'm not going to give birth in the next five minutes. You have time to get dressed, grab the bag and everything."

"You don't know that. You said it's time."

"Well, it is. But early labor takes a while."

He looks at me like I've just confessed I'm planning to climb Everest on a tricycle. He knows all these things, but in the moment they seemed to have escaped his mind.

I smile again. "I'm okay."

"You don't look in pain."

"I'm not. Yet. But we should probably go. Just in case. Oh—can you grab a snack? Just in case?" He gives me an incredulous look but tears out of the room in a way that makes me think he might just level the city trying to find me a croissant.

I waddle over to my cell phone, pull up Lev's contact, and let him know. He's technically off shift, but still in reach. Three little dots pop up, go away, pop up again... nothing yet.

Oh, how birth can bring these great men down. Eventually, Lev simply answers my text: **Congratulations. Please tell the boss I will be at the hospital.**

Who will get there first, I wonder, listening to Konstantin banging around.

The private OB team is being notified before I've even left the bedroom. My go-bag is grabbed. My coat slipped around my shoulders like I'm made of spun glass. There are several men positioned in the building, and the only one who isn't panicking holds the door open for me on my way out. He's older—Konstantin's age, or near it, and gives me a kind smile. Must be a father, maybe even a grandfather.

In the grey dawn light, Konstantin beats his driver to the curb and looks ready to murder when the man takes too long to open the door for me. I apologize, slip inside, and smile at my fiancé when he tumbles in through the other door.

It's endearing, honestly. This is a man who's faced down assassins and coup attempts with less panic than the idea of his girlfriend having a baby.

My heart swells.

He loves this child.

He loves *me*.

And as ridiculous as it is, seeing him flustered—watching him shouting into his phone in Russian—is oddly comforting.

Because I know, without a shadow of a doubt, he'll never let anything happen to us.

* * *

The hospital staff must've been warned.

We're rushed through a private entrance by a nurse who's clearly been threatened within an inch of her life to be cheerful. I'm wheeled into the VIP suite, tucked into a bed that could probably rival most luxury hotel mattresses, and handed a silky green gown with the Martynov crest stitched into the chest.

Thankfully, it's a different room than the one I was in months ago. Only a shiver of anxiety goes through me; but my focus is mostly on the baby, who is clearly trying to press here and there to find the way out.

"Jesus," I murmur as I change. "Is this what birth looks like when you're a mafia princess?"

Konstantin, sitting straight-backed in the armchair like he's preparing for war, doesn't crack a smile. His jaw is locked tight. "Queen," he corrects, then asks, "How far apart are the contractions?"

"About ten minutes. Maybe eight."

He doesn't like that answer.

The nurse—a sweet brunette named Tabitha—comes in to check my vitals. Her hands are shaking. She accidentally brushes a wire against my arm, and Konstantin shoots to his feet like it's a weapon.

"I swear to God," he growls, "if you so much as bump her wrong again, I'll have your license revoked and your retirement spent in an unheated box."

"Konstantin," I say firmly. "I need her to have functioning hands."

He doesn't sit back down.

But he does press his lips to my temple and murmur, "You shouldn't be the one in pain. Not you."

"I'm not in pain yet." It's a half-lie; the contractions aren't exactly comfortable.

"I don't care. You shouldn't be." He brushes my hair

back with one hand and lays a palm reverently on my belly. "You're everything. You hear me? Everything."

My throat tightens.

Hormones are cruel.

So is love, sometimes.

But in this moment, with his forehead pressed to mine and his hand covering the place where our son is slowly readying his entrance into the world, I feel weightless.

Like there's nothing else. Just this.

Just us.

* * *

Five hours later, I'm *definitely* in pain.

The contractions are stronger now. Closer. My back is screaming. My abdomen's clenching like it's trying to tear itself apart. Konstantin looks like he's aged ten years in the last hour, his salt-and-pepper hair dull and standing on end from running his hand through it constantly.

The nurses, aware of him but more focused on me, are serious and thorough. They've realized that *I'm* the one in control; and I need to be. Already this feels so overwhelming that I can't imagine the other side of it.

"Epidural," I pant, clutching Konstantin's hand. "I need —I need the anesthesiologist—"

"They said ten minutes. It's been fifteen," he barks at the nurse.

"I'm sorry, sir, I—"

"If you don't find someone right now," he snarls, "I *will*."

Tabitha ducks out of the room.

Konstantin leans down and strokes my face again. "You're doing beautifully."

"I am *sweating*."

"You're glowing."

"Glowing with *rage*."

He chuckles softly, and I watch the lines around his eyes crinkle. Then another contraction hits, and I crush his hand with a force that could probably dislocate a lesser man's knuckles.

He doesn't even flinch.

"Breathe, *malen'kiy volk*," he murmurs. "I've got you."

Time fractures.

Everything blurs—doctors, needles, shifting positions, the hum of a fetal monitor. The epidural helps. But then the pressure builds again. Insistent. Unrelenting.

I'm told to push.

Konstantin is at my side the entire time, one arm bracing my back, the other gripping my hand. He speaks Russian at one point, a quiet mantra I don't understand but feel in my bones. A blurry, silly thought goes through my head: at some point I should start Russian lessons, at the very least to understand his mumbling.

He's scared.

He thinks I'll break.

But I don't. Because I *have* to do this.

The pain hits a fever pitch.

I scream.

And then—a cry. Not mine, surprisingly.

A real, sharp, furious *new* cry.

Our baby.

"Congratulations," the OB says softly. "It's a boy."

The room vanishes.

All I see is the tiny, wet, furious thing placed gently on my chest. He's squalling, fists balled, face scrunched and red.

He's perfect.

Konstantin makes a sound I've never heard before. A shuddering, soft gasp. I turn to find his hand over his mouth, eyes glassy, staring like he's witnessing something sacred.

"Here," nurse Tabitha says, handing him a pair of shears. The look on her face, one raised brow—I laugh, realizing that I'm not the only one aware they're witnessing the breakdown of a powerful man.

The softening of him.

He cuts the cord with hands that only tremble slightly, then he leans down and presses the gentlest kiss in the world to our son's damp head.

"My boy," he murmurs. "My son. My little wolf."

And I cry.

I've never seen him look like this—like a man on his knees at the feet of something he worships. It's in this moment that I know that no matter what kind of world we came from, our son is going to be so, so loved.

Epilogue

6 Months Later

I walk through the glass doors of Martynov Global Holdings with a baby on my hip, a nanny trailing behind me, and the same confidence I used to fake—only now it's real.

Samuil stirs softly, blinking up at me with bleary, gray-hazel eyes. He's the spitting image of his father: sharp little brow, furrowed even in sleep, lips pursed like he's already judging the building's profit margins. He's wearing a tiny cashmere onesie and a look of vague distrust, like he's already onto the world.

Chrissy gasps when she sees me in the massive foyer. "Audrey! Are you *kidding* me right now?"

I smile and shift Sam to the other arm so I can accept the full-body hug she barrels into me with. Her hair smells like coconut and ink. It grounds me in something familiar, something good.

"Back in the flesh," I say. "I figured it was time."

She leans back and grins at Sam. "And you brought the most important Martynov of all!"

"I figured the future CEO should get a lay of the land."

Chrissy beams. "Everyone is going to lose their *minds*. Duscha especially. Did you time it for maximum dramatic effect?"

"Obviously," I deadpan. Then I touch her shoulder gently, drawing her attention. "Hey, I wanted to ask you... how would you feel about being godmother?"

Her eyes light up, then tear up. She stamps her foot with a broken laugh. "Aud! How can you do this to me at work? *Of course.*"

"Good," I mumble into another hug, this one heartfelt and strong. Since Sam's birth, Chrissy has visited a handful of times, and our friendship is even deeper. There's a thread that ties us together; the experiences we've had in the last year have drawn us together, and I can't imagine anyone else who would be a better godmother. Or understand this strange life we're living, of luxury, love, and vague danger.

The elevator pings softly as we step inside. The mirrored interior reflects back a version of me that's almost unrecognizable from the woman I was last year. My posture's straighter, my skin glows, and my expression is sharp and soft in equal measure. Am I carrying a few extra pounds? Hell yeah. Do I care? Hell no.

Motherhood hasn't dulled me. It's honed me.

And Konstantin doesn't seem to mind the extra curves *at all.*

The elevator opens on the twenty-eighth floor and Chrissy, and I step into the accounting suite like we never left—though I'm careful to pass Sam to Mila, our nanny, who falls into step behind us with quiet deference. She's former military, speaks five languages, and carries a diaper bag like it's loaded with explosives. Between her, Kashmere, and Lev, I sleep soundly at night knowing our little family is safe.

I keep my gaze ahead, confident, polished.

And then—

"Miss Wolfe."

Duscha's voice cuts through the room like a knife wrapped in frost. Her heels click across the polished floor as she approaches, the ever-present clipboard tucked beneath one arm. Her platinum hair looks dull, twisted into a bun so tight it probably registers its own gravitational pull.

I smile sweetly. "It's Mrs. Martynov now, actually."

She stops.

I see it land in her brain—the ring on my finger, the weight of the baby, the fact that I'm not just *back*, I'm *above* her now.

That the woman she tried to destroy is standing in the exact spot she tried to claw her way into.

Her mouth opens. Closes. "I wasn't informed—"

"No, I imagine you weren't." I gesture casually. "Don't worry. You'll be kept in the loop. As long as you keep your nose out of the wrong ledgers."

Duscha stiffens.

Chrissy watches the whole exchange with a look of pure glee. A second later, the internal line at the front desk buzzes.

"Mrs. Martynov," Olena's voice says. "Mr. Martynov would like to see you in his office. Bring Samuil."

Chrissy winks at me. "Show him what he's missing, baby."

I grin and nod to Mila, who hands Sam back with the care of someone passing a crown jewel.

Time to make an entrance.

* * *

Konstantin's office is the same.

But he's not.

There's a softness to him now that no one dares speak about—a warmth reserved for me, and now for the baby cradled in my arms. That ruthless edge hasn't dulled, not in the slightest, but it's wrapped in velvet now. In power that doesn't need to shout to be heard.

He stands when we enter, pushing back from the massive desk like he's been waiting all morning just to see us. I barely close the door before he's across the room.

"You're late," he murmurs.

He kisses me slowly, reverently, one hand sliding into my hair. The other settles over Sam's small back. When he pulls away, he's smiling—and only I ever get to see this version of him: the man who never stops loving, even when he's terrifying the rest of the city into submission.

"Duscha looked like she was going to implode," I add.

"She'll survive."

"She tried to ruin me."

Konstantin's mouth twitches. "And instead, she gave me everything I wanted."

That makes me laugh, low and real.

He leans down, brushes a kiss to Sam's head, and whis-

258

pers in Russian. Sam responds with a soft grunt, tiny fists curling like he's preparing to challenge God.

"He's a Martynov," Konstantin says proudly.

"He has your scowl."

"And your eyes."

I walk to the window while he watches, adjusting Sam's blanket. The city stretches out before us, distant and glittering. Everything feels sharp and full. This life is nothing I imagined—and somehow, more than I ever dared hope for.

"He's scheduled for feeding at noon," I say absently. "And then a nap."

"I'll reschedule my meeting," he murmurs behind me.

When I turn, he's watching us like we're something holy.

I feel the heat of his gaze slide down my body, slow and hungry.

"You wore that dress on purpose," he says.

"It's my first day back. I wanted to set the tone."

He's quiet a moment, then says softly, "It's hard to watch you walk back into this place. Not because I'm angry. But because I'm afraid of what the world might try to take from me."

"You've already made me untouchable," I remind him. "Everyone knows. And everyone's scared of you. Or trying to be friends. Fia invited us to dinner this weekend."

"Mmm... tell her we'll consider it."

I roll my eyes, giving him a smirk, and walk back over to settle Sam into the bassinet near the window—one of Konstantin's personal additions to the office. It's sleek, dark gray, and cost more than my first car. "I already told her yes."

For a few minutes, we're quiet as Sam settles in. It's times like these that Lev is indispensable; he makes the perfect, killer babysitter, and Konstantin and I have learned from him.

"Thank you," I say softly, turning toward my husband.

He frowns. "For what?"

"For letting me come back. For trusting me. For treating me like I'm still my own person."

He closes the space between us and takes my chin between two fingers.

"I don't let you do anything," he says, voice low. "You are my wife. The mother of my child. And you've earned your place in this empire. Don't forget that."

Hearing it is a balm.

He releases my chin and circles behind me, pressing his body to mine. I feel the heat of him through the silk of my dress, the steady hum of his breath at the base of my neck.

"When we get home," he says, voice like silk and sin, "we're going to celebrate your return."

"Oh? How?"

"I'm going to undress you slowly. Kiss every inch of your skin. Remind you who you belong to. And then I'm going to fuck you so well you forget what numbers are."

My breath catches, and a laugh tumbles out.

"Maybe I *want* to remember numbers," I tease. "I did just start back at work. Don't forget—you need me, Konstantin."

He laughs against my throat.

"Don't I know it."

A small sound gurgles from the bassinet, and we both turn instantly. Sam stirs, eyes cracking open, looking around like he's already plotting how to buy out his rivals' shares before snack time.

Konstantin walks over and picks him up with startling ease.

"You're getting heavy, little wolf," he murmurs, adjusting Sam in one arm. "Your mother keeps feeding you like you're training for war."

I lean against the window, watching them.

This is my life now.

This man.

This child.

This place.

I'm not afraid anymore. I know who I am now, and I know what I've survived. I've walked through hell in heels and came out holding the hand of the devil who chose me over the world.

Sam coos softly, one chubby fist reaching toward my face. I press a kiss to his knuckles. Then another to Konstantin's lips.

"Let's go home," I whisper.

He grins.

"Yes, *malen'kiy volk*. Let's go home."

THE END

Read more from Sierra Voss with the Prince's Guild series. Available on Amazon.

Printed in Dunstable, United Kingdom